# OUTLAW CANYON

Rafe and Seth Laramie were just trying to go home, but, mistakenly targeted by an angry posse, they are forced to flee a hail of bullets and hide out in the town of Greybull. There, the enigmatic Mort Sangster helps them to evade the posse. But all is not as it seems. The brothers follow Sangster to his cabin where outlaws, plotting an elaborate crime, invite them into the fold . . . but what bloody battles lie ahead if they accept?

*Books by Jack Sheriff*
*in the Linford Western Library:*

JACK SHERIFF

# OUTLAW CANYON

*Complete and Unabridged*

## LINFORD
*Leicester*

First published in Great Britain in 2011 by
Robert Hale Limited
London

First Linford Edition
published 2012
by arrangement with
Robert Hale Limited
London

British Library CIP Data

Sheriff, Jack, *1936* –
    Outlaw canyon. - -
    (Linford western library)
    1. Brothers- -Fiction. 2. Criminals- -
    Fiction. 3. Western stories.
    4. Large type books.
    I. Title II. Series
    823.9'2–dc23

    ISBN 978–1–4448–1096–7

Published by
F. A. Thorpe (Publishing)
Anstey, Leicestershire

Set by Words & Graphics Ltd.
Anstey, Leicestershire
Printed and bound in Great Britain by
T. J. International Ltd., Padstow, Cornwall

# PART ONE

# THE POSSE

# 1

When Rafe Laramie sent the coffee pot's dregs hissing onto the fire's dying embers, the dawn chill was coating the western foothills with glistening silvery dew, the sun still a distant promise endowing the southern peaks of the Bighorn Mountains with rims of gold.

Rafe, well over six feet tall, looked as wide as a barn door against the early morning light. As he moved away from the acrid reek of the dying fire and began rolling his bedding, he was determined to keep pushing his objections. He knew his arguments were weak and without substance, yet the forebodings would not go away. That meant if talking didn't change Seth's mind, he'd need to use force. He felt his muscles tightening with tension as he looked across at his brother.

'I can't see any good coming out of

it, that's why,' he said. 'Besides, I can't see the point in visiting a Wyoming town we don't know, for a reason you haven't yet dreamed up, when it's going to take us miles out of our way.'

Younger brother Seth was just as stubborn.

'The reason is I can see Alamo down there. The Bighorn River's shrouded in mist, but that town's roofs are beckoning to me like the golden towers of ancient Babylon — and if that's too flowery for you, then how about this: we've been too long on the trail. In the past few days we've come down from the Laramie Mountains, crossed the North Platte, crossed the Powder, crossed Crazy Woman Creek. Last night we pushed through Powder River Pass, then slept rough — like we have every night for the past, what, six months? — and I've had enough. I need a shave, I stink like an old hog — '

'Yeah,' Rafe said quickly, seeing the opening. 'I've been telling you that for days, Seth. My concern is, you look so bad I'm scared if you set foot in any town people will take you for a bank robber. If that happens I'll be wasting even more time talking you out of a jail cell.'

Seth, stocky and muscular, paused in the act of saddling his blue roan.

'You mean you *are* considering going there? You're backing down?'

'No, that's not what I'm doing,' Rafe said, glaring. 'All right, the idea of a hot bath is appealing. I'm sick to death of jerky. The food we've been dishing up is either a greasy mess, or something only a horse could chew. My mouth's watering even now at the thought of a thick steak sizzling in a clean pan. But that bit about you getting arrested was only part jesting. I told you I smell trouble. Instinct's telling me to steer clear of Alamo, so what I'm doing is working hard to make you see sense.'

Seth shook his head. He settled the saddle, and bent to tighten the cinch. When he straightened up, he was frowning.

'We've already been through a heap of trouble in the two years since we left southern Texas, and we've always come out on top. We've out-gunned drunken cowboys who figured shooting us was more fun than drilling holes in a few false fronts. Got out of smoky New Mexico cantinas with our hides still unperforated when the odds were telling us we hadn't a hope in hell.' He nodded pointedly at Rafe. 'And we've also bested mean fellows who'd fought on the side of the North and took exception to the pale colour of your army jacket — '

'Yours too, you're still wearing it and we were on the same side — '

'So maybe it was that you've got the smell of officer about you and any fool can see I was an enlisted man — '

'Or maybe more than a few we fell foul of got all fired up by that belligerent attitude you have, that side of your nature that won't let you forget you're not still fighting a war.'

'Yeah, maybe,' Seth said reluctantly.

He stepped back from his horse and stood with hands on hips. 'OK, you've made your point in a dozen different ways, and I'm getting tired of arguing. I don't agree with you, can't understand why you want to avoid Alamo when we both stink to high heaven and look like drifters who've been trampled in the mud by a herd of rogue steers. But in another couple of weeks we'll be home, seven long years after we rode out to seek our fortunes. We never did manage that. Instead we wound up wearin' ourselves out fighting in a four-year war, and now I aim to get home in one piece. If that means staying out of trouble — even if for the life of me I can't see where that trouble's coming from — then I'm willing to try.'

'Trying's not needed, Seth. All we do is stay out of trouble spots.'

'For Christ's sake, Alamo's nothing more than a small town on the Bighorn.'

'Instinct's telling me otherwise,' Rafe said bluntly. 'And if you hadn't backed down, staying away from Alamo would have been an order, by the way — and don't forget I outranked you in the war, and I outrank you now in family seniority.'

'But never in brains.' The muscles in Seth's jaw were bunched. 'And let me tell you, big Brother, you'll never know how close those last stupid remarks about me backing down came to making me dig in my heels till hell froze over.'

Disgruntled, but finally prepared to accept defeat, he turned away with a dark look in his eyes that clearly told Rafe to accept what he'd got, and back off.

They finished breaking camp together. By the time they mounted up and started their horses down the rocky slopes leading to the beckoning grass-lands, the sun had risen above the mountains to warm their backs and was lifting the mist off the Bighorn River.

★ ★ ★

Their route took them due west through lush green cattle country sandwiched between the still-shaded Bighorn Mountains at their backs, the hazy, sundrenched Rocky Mountains some eighty miles away to their front. By midday their horses were splashing through the Nowood, a tributary of the Bighorn River, spray kicked up by dancing hoofs glistening like cascades of glittering jewels in the sunlight.

Once across the river, Rafe decreed that they take a well-earned break. After swilling their faces in the icy river they ate a meal of cold jerky washed down with lukewarm water from their canteens, then stretched out — well apart, for Seth was still grumbling — on the river-bank in the dappled shade of a stand of aspen.

At noon on that hot summer's day both Rafe and Seth fell asleep and slept like drunken 'punchers, the impromptu break dragging on long enough to wipe out most of the afternoon. Rafe stirred first. He squinted through the trees and saw Seth flat on his back and snoring into his Stetson in the lengthening shadows. A glance at the sun told him they must have slept for four hours, and he shook his head in disbelief. Then, yawning, he looked with misgivings at ominous storm clouds gathering over the Bighorn Mountains and, without haste, climbed to his feet and began preparing to move off.

Eventually Seth regained consciousness. When he was back in the saddle, slack of limb, bleary-eyed but ready to go, Rafe pointed them towards the north and led the way at a steady canter along the Nowood's grassy bank. They were following the direction indicated by a trail that lay in the open a little to their left, but were able to slip in and out of the shade of groves of cottonwoods straggling along the edge of the river. The scent of the water, clean and cool as it flowed over a mostly rocky bed, was causing their mounts to prick their ears and try to slow the pace.

An hour later, Seth, making a great

show of sniffing the air, swore he could smell the town of Alamo and began casting imploring glances in Rafe's direction. A short while after that, Rafe looked keenly ahead and realized at once that he'd slipped up.

'Dammit,' he said, drawing rein. 'Do you see what I see? We got ourselves a soaking up to the waist crossing that river back there — and we had no need to. That trail leads arrow straight to Alamo; the town's sitting snug in the fork where the Nowood shoots off south-east from the Bighorn. To avoid it we should've followed the east bank of that pesky river. Now we've got to cross back over.'

'Or,' Seth said, 'now you've got us this close to the town — '

'No, sir,' Rafe said, jaw tight. 'That choppy water a couple of hundred yards ahead tells me there's a wide ridge rising close to the surface. Just there it'll be shallow enough to cross without getting soaked again, and that's what we'll do.'

Seth took the rebuff in silence. Rafe touched his horse with his heels and urged it down the bank. The slope was gentle. The river was lapping the shiny mud and coarse shingle at the edge of the grass, and Rafe let his grateful horse splash its way upriver through the shallows.

Then, without warning, their luck began to run out like grain from a split sack.

'Riders heading this way, from Alamo,' Seth called. 'Two of 'em, riding like the Devil's on their heels.'

Rafe glanced back. His brother had held his roan to the firmer ground higher up the bank, and so had a better view. Vaguely uneasy, Rafe pushed on, still looking sideways and up the slope. A few seconds more and the sound of hoofs reached his ears above the splash and hiss of the water. Then Seth was easing his roan down the bank. He came up behind Rafe as the two riders thundered on by. Rapidly, the drum of hoofs faded into a dying whisper of sound.

Seth pulled alongside Rafe. His eyes, Rafe noticed, were darting nervously, his face set.

'I think you were right about that town,' Seth said. 'What I smell now is trouble. We're on the wrong side of the river, big Brother, let's make for that ford you spotted.'

'D'you get a good look at those two?'

'Enough. Rough, unshaven, armed to the teeth. It's a fine summer's day. Where we're at now is an earthly paradise, so why were they riding like they couldn't wait to get away?'

'Don't let it bother you. Another five minutes, with luck we'll be out of here.'

Using the word luck without any premonition of what was to come, his own words scarcely registering before they floated away on the warm breeze, Rafe urged his horse to a canter. With Seth again keeping the roan higher up the bank on his left, they reached the choppy water Rafe had spotted. There he turned his horse hard right and took it into the river. The submerged bank causing the water to break up was composed of shifting stones on packed sand, just beneath the surface. Followed closely by Seth, Rafe kept his horse splashing across the Nowood with the level of the fast-flowing water steady between fetlock and hock, the gouts of water kicked up by the horses barely touching his boots.

Behind him, Seth gave a shrill, nervous yip of relief as they spurred their mounts up the far bank, pushed them away from the river and into the longer grass and again turned towards the north. Unaccountably, Rafe was feeling the same sense of trouble left behind that had been evident in Seth's gleeful shout. There was the urge within him to push his horse to greater speed — yet he knew that was unreasonable. The foreboding that had come over Seth had been his, Rafe's doing. He had planted in his brother's mind the fear of the unknown, and the unexpected had caused him to panic. But the reality was that nothing extraordinary had happened. Two riders in a hurry had passed them, two men they had never seen before and would never see again —

'More riders,' Seth called, and now there was naked apprehension in the unnaturally high pitch of his voice. 'Coming fast from the direction of Alamo, like those others were. They're waving and pointing this way — pointing at us.'

Even as he called out, spurred the roan rapidly alongside Rafe and rode straight on by, the faint, ringing cries of the men on the other side of the river reached Rafe's ears. Giving his horse its head, he adjusted his position to the rapidly increasing gait, then twisted in the saddle to look back.

A short way upstream from the ford, riders were pouring down the Nowood's west bank and kicking up brilliant fountains of spray as they rode hard through the deeper water. In their efforts to get across the river they had spread out into a line, lifted their rifles clear of the water, and stopped shouting to save their breath. But in the few seconds that he spent watching their relentless pursuit — for, surely, that was what he was witnessing — Rafe was hit hard by a bolt of spine-tingling terror that left him fearing for his life. It was as if the fury within the riders was carried to him in rolling waves. Feeling a constriction in his chest, overwhelmed by raw emotions he could not comprehend, Rafe turned away and spurred after Seth.

Yet the last brief glimpse he had of that terrifying posse — dammit, Rafe thought, why did that word come to mind? — confirmed his worst fears. The lead rider threw caution to the winds. Standing in his stirrups, gripping his horse's barrel with knees that were deep in the cold, swirling waters, he rammed his rifle butt into his shoulder and fired a string of fast shots towards Rafe and Seth.

They came too close to be healthy. Bullets kicked up dirt between Seth's roan's flying hoofs. Others clipped leaves from the trees as the brothers tore around a bend and tucked in tight to a steep bank leading up into the woods over which hung dark purple clouds. Then the trail narrowed, thick forest encroaching on either side. For several long minutes, it was as if the two of them were alone in that part of Wyoming. All about them as they rode at a furious pace there was the thunder of hoofs, the jingle of harness, the creak of leather, the ragged rasp of breathing. But those sounds were theirs: their horses' hoofs; their pulses hammering in their ears; and those familiar sounds were comforting.

It couldn't last.

'When they're across the river they'll come after us hard and fast,' Rafe yelled. 'We've got to figure a way out of this, or we're dead men.'

'Dead by mistake, which is no consolation,' Seth shouted back. 'That posse — '

'Is that what it is?'

'Well, they're hunting down some-body — and they've got it wrong; they saw us crossing the river and jumped to the wrong conclusion. I reckon they've got us confused with those two we saw heading south, but I don't aim to turn around and get into a heated discus-sion.'

The posse, Rafe noted with a snatched glance over his shoulder, was still out of sight around the bend. On that narrow trail, there was scarcely room for two riders abreast, so they would be strung out. As he faced front again, from the clouds that had settled over the mountains and rolled down the foothills dark blobs of rain began to fall. Swiftly, that spatter of heavy droplets turned into a downpour. As if someone had opened a sluice gate the deluge at once cut visibility to a hundred yards; the wind, strengthening by the minute, was driving the rain, shaking water from the clattering trees and carrying aloft the fine spray from the rain bouncing on the trail.

Within Rafe's breast, hope surged.

'Listen to me, Seth,' he called, pulling his horse back to a steady trot. 'We crossed the Nowood twice, now we're going to do it a third time. There's a whole crowd of them chasing us up a narrow trail — too many. I reckon they'll be losing ground, and I know for sure a couple of river crossings coming after the one they've just done will slow them more than us — '

'A *couple* of crossings?'

'That's right. We going to cross to the Nowood's west bank, just to the north of Alamo. If we do it sudden, where they can't see us, they'll not realize we've turned off and ride straight on by.'

'That's one crossing,' Seth said, waiting.

'A short ride west from the Nowood we'll hit the outer bend of an ox-bow on the Big Horn river. We cross that, end up in that loop, they'll be wondering what the hell's going on and where we're going next.'

'Yeah, like I am.'

Rafe grinned bleakly across at Seth through the rainwater pouring from his hat brim.

'There's a town some way to the north. Called Greybull. We need somewhere to hole up. That posse's riding strung out now, those behind the lead man eating the mud and water he's kicking up in their faces. If we can make it to Greybull ahead of them — '

A rifle cracked behind them, the report distorted into waves of sound by the violence of the downpour. In the deafening roar of the rain and the noise of their horses splashing through muddy water deepening in ruts and potholes, there was no way of telling where the bullet finished up. Rafe guessed the gunman was firing without hope of a hit, and didn't bother looking over his shoulder.

'Move it,' he shouted and, putting spurs to his horse, he again began to widen the gap between pursuers and pursued.

They rode abreast, the two brothers, the water and muddy spray kicked up by their horses flying harmlessly away to their rear. They rode in a dream world, for the light was eerie. The sun was already low in the west between the black peaks of the Rocky Mountains and the dark, hanging hem that was the edge of the lowering purple rain clouds. Its red glow was reflected from the clouds' underbelly to be diffused by the rain which, on the western side of the trail, was transformed into a pale red mist.

They were riding through a raging storm. Rafe was working out their position by guesswork. He could judge the speed of their horses, but was unable to get a glimpse of Alamo. All he knew for certain was that they were pulling away from the posse. Not far enough to lose them, but all he needed was enough space to evade them — temporarily.

That came when there was a sudden lull in the storm, and a snatched backward glance revealed an empty trail.

'We'll cross here!' he shouted.

Without slackening pace, using his knees and the strength of his hands on the reins, he wrenched his mount to the left so violently the animal almost lost its footing in the slick mud. Rafe leaned back in the saddle as the horse slid with braced legs down a steep bank. He felt his teeth snap together as it hit bottom, then again used his spurs to keep it moving fast across a long grassy slope.

Once out of the trees, the full force of the wind hit him. A westerly gale was driving up the river. The rain was needle-sharp, the grass flattened by wind and rain and as slippery underfoot as wet cowhide. But the river was close. With one swift glance back to make sure Seth was following, Rafe covered the last few yards at the gallop and took his horse straight down the bank and into the water.

The fierce wind was whipping the surface of the river into a choppy foam.

This time there was no submerged ridge to provide footing, and horse and rider had entered the water where the bed shelved steeply. The horse, stretching its neck, hit with a tremendous splash and went straight under. When it surfaced, eyes rolling, nostrils flared, Rafe slid from the saddle into the deep water. Holding on to the slippery horn with one hand, he kicked out. Half swimming, half dragged through the water by the gallant horse, he squinted through the rain and the foam and watched with fear in his heart as the west bank very gradually drew closer.

Then the current began to pull them downstream.

The manageable thirty-yard crossing stretched to fifty, then sixty, and still they hadn't reached the far bank. Tiring, the horse's kicks weakened, became feeble, and it began to wallow without making any progress. Cursing himself for leaving his boots on, Rafe kicked and pulled himself forward far enough for the struggling animal to see him. Then, saying a silent prayer, he relinquished his grip on the horn. Clinging fiercely to the reins he managed to swim until he was ahead of the horse. He was fighting the ice-cold water, coughing and spluttering, gasping for breath as foaming crests were driven into his face. But with the reins stretched tight, horse and man were again moving in the right direction — but very slowly, and Rafe could feel the strength draining rapidly from his limbs. He couldn't tell if he was pulling the horse, or if his presence was reviving the animal and it was moving. All he knew was that the threads that held them to life were close to snapping, and the west bank was still ten yards away.

Then his kicking feet hit bottom. They'd reached the shallows.

Emitting a gasping, strangled yell of triumph that was caught and whipped away by the wind, he splashed and floundered his way towards the bank. He was still hauling on the reins. The horse struggled after him. Revived by Rafe's infectious excitement, it whinnied shrilly. Then, moving jerkily, water streaming from its slick hide, it went past Rafe and stood trembling on the grassy bank.

Only then, as he reached the horse and bent forward with his hands on his braced thighs and his chest heaving, did Rafe remember his brother and look anxiously back at the river.

Seth was in trouble.

Halfway across he had followed Rafe's example and slid from the saddle to take his weight off the horse. But the roan had weakened rapidly. Battling against wind, rain and current, it had given up the fight and was drifting downstream, taking Seth with him.

Swiftly, Rafe turned to his horse and undid the strap holding his rawhide lariat. Then he ran along the bank. Shaking out a loop while running, watching Seth and the roan as he rapidly gained on them and at last drew level, he slipped on the slick grass and fell flat on his back.

His head cracked against a half-buried rock. A bolt of lightning in his brain blotted out the storm. Then, shaking his head to banish the red blotches, he rolled over and regained his feet.

Seth was fighting a losing battle. He was swimming with a strong side stroke, hauling on the reins to try to turn the roan's head towards the bank. But his attempts to save the horse were pulling its head under the choppy water. Panicking, the roan was jerking its head to free itself — and, as Rafe watched in horror, the reins were ripped from Seth's hands.

With cold, fumbling fingers, Rafe found the end of his lariat and took a dally around a slender cottonwood, turning the trunk into a makeshift snubbing post. Then he stepped down the bank, whirled the loop around his head and made his throw.

It fell short, splashed uselessly onto the river's choppy surface and sank.

Hand over hand, Rafe hauled in the now heavy rawhide, all the while squinting across the water to gauge the distance. He had been standing still. Even in those few seconds the current had taken the horse further downstream. Seth, meanwhile, was gallantly swimming after his mount, but falling behind.

'Ease off!' Rafe yelled, and felt his words whipped away by the wind. 'Save your strength, stay afloat, drift in to the bank.'

He was running as he shouted. He saw Seth's white face as he twisted in the water and lifted a hand in acknowledgement. Then, again level with the drowning horse, Rafe made his second throw.

The loop sailed towards the roan. For an instant it seemed as if the wind would carry it away to one side. Then it settled neatly over the saddle horn. Rafe jerked it tight. Once he was sure it was secure, he released the lariat and backed away. It was running out rapidly. As he stepped over it and away from the river-bank, the rawhide snapped taut. The dally around the cottonwood held. At the other end of the lariat, the roan's drift downstream was halted with a jerk.

Seth had made it to the bank. He struggled out of the river, his clothes streaming water as he came erect. His head was turned, his eyes on the roan. Reading the situation at a glance, he stepped over the taut rope and spun around to take hold of it. Rafe was already hauling on it with both hands. Working together, heels dug in as they pulled sideways on rope as hard and as stiff as an iron bar, they worked the roan in towards the bank.

'It'll make it,' Seth said through his teeth. 'It's a lazy son-of-a-bitch. You watch, it feels solid ground beneath its feet it'll be out like a shot.'

And so it proved. The glistening roan came up out of the water with head held high and eyes flashing, and trotted along the bank. Reaching Seth, it shook itself, stood stiff-legged and shivering. Rafe removed his lariat from the saddle-horn and coiled it. Seth stayed with the roan, soothing it with gentle hands. He was staring out across the river.

'The storm's slackening, it'll be done in a while,' he said. 'If that posse rode on by like you said, by now they'll've realized their mistake.'

But Rafe was already moving. He jogged to his horse, buckled his lariat in place then swung into the saddle. Seth followed suit. Rafe waited until his brother brought the rejuvenated roan alongside, then flicked the reins and together they headed west away from the Nowood. As they did so, Rafe's final backward glance told him they were just in time.

'First man's there, watching,' he gritted. 'The others'll be quick to join him.'

'We didn't give them the slip, and they'll have better conditions when they cross,' Seth said. 'That storm lost us what we'd gained.'

'But not enough to do them much good.' Through the now fine rain illuminated by the last rays of the setting sun, Rafe grinned across at his brother. 'The Big Horn's not too far away. We'll be there before they've crossed the Nowood, across that ox-bow and making the run for Greybull before they've shaken the water out of their ears.'

# 2

Lake Rafferty was in a vile temper.

He was sitting hunched on a log with smoke burning his eyes, wet right through to his skin, chilled to the bone, and his head was spinning from the frequent twists and turns his partner had decreed necessary if they were to escape the posse. OK, so he'd been proved right — so far. But in Rafferty's opinion they would have made it anyway if they'd headed north after robbing the Alamo bank. Instead they'd turned due south, damn near drowned in a violent summer storm, and in the end escaped the posse's wrath by a stroke of pure luck.

'You picked out any more fast flowin' rivers we can go swimmin' in?' he called.

Milo Crane shook his head. He was thirty yards away, scouting for dry brushwood along the fringe of the woods encircling the clearing. The fire he'd managed to get going using wet kindling was sending a plume of white smoke into the evening sky. For a few brief moments he'd worried about it being spotted by the posse. Then, remembering what he had witnessed, he'd dismissed those fears.

'Not so's you'd notice,' he called. 'When we get there, there's a trickle of a creek to the south of Greybull — but you know all about that one. Before today I've seen you put your horse to it and go flying across in a single bound.'

'That rain storm we came through can turn a creek into a torrent,' Rafferty snapped.

'It's heading west, and dying,' Crane said, 'same as that bank teller you plugged.'

'Don't blame me for that,' Rafferty snarled. 'He was hangin' onto that cash like it was his own. Also, he had a shotgun under the counter and was about to blast you straight through the woodwork.'

'True, and your speedy intervention's appreciated. But now we're wanted killers, with a rope waiting to stretch our necks if we're caught.'

'As we're working for Mort Sangster,' Rafferty said, 'there's no chance of that happening. He tells us he's an important man. If that's right, and we just got all the ready cash he needs at considerable risk to our skins, he'll see us OK.'

Crane walked towards the smouldering fire, dumped the few broken branches he'd picked up onto the wet earth, then shook his head.

'I haven't got your blind faith in that puffed-up, pompous, bastard Rafferty. It occurred to me some time ago that once we hand over that cash you've got in your saddle-bags, it's in Sangster's interests to get rid of us.'

Rafferty grinned mirthlessly.

'I don't trust him any more than you do, but I know there's more to him than meets the eye,' he said. 'Didn't he tell us this Alamo robbery is the first step in a major undertaking? — whatever the hell that means.'

He carefully placed the fresh fuel on the fire, poked with a stick and watched a flame burst forth and begin licking at the logs. Crane, meanwhile, had dug a coffee pot out of his saddle-bags, and within a short while the pot was suspended over a blazing fire and rich black java was bubbling.

For some time, as they drank that fresh coffee from tin cups clutched in both hands, there was a comfortable silence. Both men huddled close to the flames. They were dressed in the ordinary garb of a working cowboy, though every item of clothing they wore was now wrinkled and stained from the fierce storm they had endured.

That ordinary appearance was Crane's doing.

Milo Crane was an ageing villain — though nobody said that to his face —

with a lined countenance under steel-grey hair and eyes that gave nothing away. In his many years of crime he had always adhered to one maxim, the merits of which he had expounded at length around countless camp-fires.

'If you're going to commit robbery,' he would say, 'then don't ride into town looking like a villain, or a villain is what you'll be taken for — and taken, as likely as not, long before you get anywhere near the bank. Make sense? Of course it does.'

He was also wont to say, as a clincher, 'If you adhere to that code of ethics, my sons' — this said with a suitably deadpan expression — 'you'll live to experience the same success I've enjoyed, and the riches that go with it.'

Inevitably, those last words were greeted with stunned silence, then an explosion of laughter led by Crane himself as he stood in the flickering firelight and passed the whiskey jug.

As Crane now fondly recalled those fleeting, pleasant moments, he stared with some misgivings across the fire at his trigger-happy partner.

Rafferty's temper had cooled even as his clothes steamed in the heat, but it was that temper and his itchy trigger finger that had got them into deep trouble. Watching him, Crane thought back over the past few hours that had seen them ride into the town of Alamo, rob the bank, seen Rafferty plug a man stone dead when the necessity for such an action was in doubt, then leave at a dead run with a posse snapping at their heels.

And it was soon after that, Crane mused, that there had been a most unusual and heartening development.

'I wonder,' he mused, 'who those two fellows were?'

Rafferty's grin was wolfish.

'Don't matter none. They pulled that posse away from us, and clear across the river. With luck they'll be swinging from a tall tree with their eyes bugged out. That puts us in the clear.'

'No. They'll have pleaded innocence.

When the posse can't find the bank's money, they'll realize they've hanged the wrong men. They'll double back, come looking for us.'

'Yeah, you could be right. In that case, it'd be better if those fellers got clear away when the storm broke,' Rafferty said. 'The posse'll press on after them, all the time putting miles between us and them.'

'Meanwhile,' Crane said, 'we've got a decision to make. Do we bed down here for the night, or push on to Greybull at the risk of treading on that posse's tail and starting the chase all over again?'

'Push on,' Rafferty said, climbing to his feet and stretching his long arms to the night skies. 'I ain't sleepin' out here in the open, and I've already told you that posse's long gone.'

'I'm pleased you're so damn certain,' Crane said, the sarcasm lost on Rafferty.

'Damn right,' Rafferty said. 'Those two fellers're running for their life.

They'll drag that posse halfway to Montana, leaving the way clear for us to ride into Greybull, hand the money over to Sangster and collect our cut.'

'Yeah,' Crane said, his mind chasing possibilities as he rose and began absently kicking dirt over the fire. 'You know, Sangster never did tell us what he wants all that cash for. That major undertaking you mentioned could have something in it for us. I can't wait to find out exactly what he's up to.'

# 3

Much to Rafe Laramie's relief, the misfortune that had dogged them since crossing the Nowood with the posse breathing down their necks seemed to have drifted west with the storm. They crossed the Big Horn's ox-bow without incident, left the spit of land that was caught in the river's loop and began pushing on towards Greybull.

The town, Rafe knew, nestled in the confluence of the Big Horn and Greybull rivers — so there would probably be one more river crossing. That realization caused him to cast an amused glance at his brother; for the past thirty minutes Seth had been bitterly expressing the view that one more soaking would see flesh and bone permanently waterlogged.

From the ox-bow to Greybull was a ride of some twenty miles. In daylight, with good conditions and fresh horses, they would have been looking at less than two hours. But Seth's roan, weakened by the Nowood crossing, was tiring rapidly. The torrential downpour had left the ground soggy, and the riders were forced constantly to hunt for firmer going as both horses began to flag. Trouble was, that resulted in their spending as much time working their way back and forth as they did pushing ahead. As that effort began to take its toll and the pace dropped almost to a crawl, Rafe began to cast frequent worried glances over his shoulder.

The storm's low pressure system had dragged the heavy clouds with it. As they slid away to the west, chasing the fleeing sun, an early moon floated in clear skies. By its light Rafe caught the occasional glimpse of the posse: from higher ground the glint of bright metal way back on the winding trail would catch his eye, or objects would pass in front of moonlit pools and, in that instant, reveal themselves by blocking the reflected light.

He'd also spotted movement in another direction, a disturbing fact he hadn't yet communicated to Seth.

'Still there on our tail, but as far as I can tell they're no closer,' he said at last, an unconvincing observation that was blurted more for his own reassurance than Seth's.

'Don't worry, old man,' Seth said with a rare grin. 'You're watching the back-trail by moonlight, I'm looking ahead; maybe that reveals something about our characters. Look, we rode straight past the town of Basin a half-hour ago. If I'm not mistaken, the lights I can see ahead must be Greybull.'

'I may be older than you, but that says something else about our characters: when I worry now, it's for a damn good reason. While you've been watching your front, I've been tracking that posse's movements. I hate to tell you this, but a couple of 'em were left behind on the far bank. For a reason.

Out of the crowd, they can ride faster, and are less likely to lose us.'

'And they're over there now?'

'They are. Saw them five minutes ago. Out from under the trees and riding like bats out of hell. If I was a real worrier, I'd say they were trying to get ahead of us.'

'Let them,' Seth said. 'We can get lost in Greybull.'

'A mouse couldn't get lost in that town,' Rafe said. 'One main street, a few businesses, a barn, a saloon ... ' He shrugged. 'Heading there seemed like a good idea when we were in the middle of that storm — hell, *anywhere* dry seemed better than where we were then. Now ... ? Well, I've got the feeling we could be riding to a town where we could too easily get boxed in.'

Seth had eased back, and both horses were walking. He looked questioningly at Rafe.

'Change of plan?'

For a moment, Rafe hesitated. Then he shook his head.

'No. I still believe we'll get there ahead of those two fellows racing up the far bank. If we get rid of the horses in the livery barn — tuck 'em up in stalls for the night — there's a chance we can lose ourselves in the crowd.'

'A crowd,' Seth mocked, 'in a town where a mouse stands no chance of hiding?'

Rafe grinned. 'I never yet rode into a town at night where there wasn't a few drinkers bellied up at the saloon bar.'

'Drinkers, sure,' Seth said doubtfully, 'but every small town I've come across treats strangers like they've got the plague.'

'If that's the case,' Rafe said, 'we'll just have to use our natural charm.'

★   ★   ★

They did have one more river to cross. The one consolation — in Rafe's opinion — was that the Greybull river that lay across their path was a shallow creek compared to the Bighorn river

43

that lay in wait for the two fast-riding members of the posse.

They crossed without incident. Water pouring down from the hills after the recent storm was threatening to turn a trickle into a roaring spate, but that would come in the hours before dawn. Even Seth conceded that the crossing was unlikely to leave him waterlogged, and by the time they turned towards the town of Greybull there was little to show that they had made three river crossings in as many hours.

In that mountainous part of the west the fertile land lay close to the many rivers, and especially the Bighorn. Their approach to the town saw them riding in from wooded slopes leading down to lush meadows, trees and fields, all bathed in cold moonlight. Mist, hanging over the Bighorn, drifted like gunsmoke lingering over the cold corpses of long dead soldiers.

Their pace was deliberately casual, the look of weariness in their faces and bearing perfectly natural. They slumped tiredly in the saddle as they entered town — exaggerating the effect, but not over-doing it, as Rafe had suggested to Seth. Oil lamps hung from rusty brackets, creaking in the soft breeze. Those lamps cast their yellow light on to the uneven plank walks on the edges of a broad, moonlit street that was simply a space between buildings hastily erected by the first arrivals, who began sawing timber where they halted their wagons.

Most of the lamplight came from the saloon, a building with a peeling sign that proclaimed it to be the Greybull Palace.

'If there's a palace,' Rafe remarked as they rode by, 'that means there's a king.'

'If there's a king,' Seth said, 'we won't find him in there.'

'Maybe he's a would-be king in search of a kingdom,' Rafe said with a sideways grin, 'seeing as we're making up stories as we go.'

Despite the banter, both men were

keeping their ears cocked for the furious sound of riders approaching the town. So they rode down the wide street fully alert, aware of eyes watching them from outside the saloon, of a stone-built structure with barred windows that was undoubtedly the jail. A light gleamed in that window.

'If the town marshal's in there, he'll join in the fun,' Seth said, 'when it starts.'

'I want to be out of here before that happens,' Rafe said.

Seth shot him a perplexed glance.

'First you said this was where we were going to hole up. Then you said a mouse couldn't get lost here, and we could be riding ourselves into a box. Yet still we came here — and now you want to leave.'

'D'you ever believe in fate?'

They'd pulled up in front of the broad, open doors of Greybull's livery barn. Rafe was swinging out of the saddle as he asked the question. He paused, feet firmly planted on the dusty street, hands folded on the horn as he looked across at Seth.

'Nope, not ever,' Seth said, 'and now's not the ideal time to begin.'

'We'll see.'

With those cryptic words, Rafe led the way inside the barn. At once he stepped out of cold moonlight and into a warmer world of horses and rustling straw, where the sheen of leather and the glint of metal fitments reflected the light of a single oil lamp suspended from a bracket outside a sagging office cubicle. The door was open. Rafe could see a pair of legs, ankles crossed where they rested on a chair without a back; could hear the rasping snores of the old hostler, who slept and dreamed his dreams.

For it was always an old man, Rafe mused, as he moved down the runway, his horse nudging his shoulder with his warm muzzle. Oftentimes the livery barn was where a wrangler ended up when he'd ridden one bronc too many, when joints began to tear apart instead of mend, when the ache of frequently broken bones became too painful to bear.

*He deals now with gentler steeds in a kinder environment,* Rafe thought, *so let him sleep with his memories* — and then he came to an abrupt halt and felt Seth bump into his back as he realized they were being watched.

A tall man was standing with his back against the split, warped timber of the far wall. Moonlight seeped through the chinks, making a halo of crinkly white hair but putting his face and body in shadow. He had been down on one knee in the sawdust on the other side of a big palomino gelding, tightening a saddle cinch. It had been the clink of the metal, the squeak of the strap, that had alerted Rafe.

Now the man was standing, leaning with his elbows on the saddle as he watched Rafe.

'You boys must have been driven there by the storm,' he said in a voice that was deep and mellow. 'Or has something more pressing brought you to this Godforsaken hole?'

He came around the horse, his hand trailing across its neck. The lamp's flame touched him with faint yellow light, picked out the planes of his face. He had an aquiline nose, blue eyes under eyebrows as white as his hair. His broad shoulders strained at a buckskin jacket. Dark pants were tucked into tan leather boots, and a pistol with a yellowed ivory butt hung low on his right thigh. It was tied down with a rawhide thong.

Rafe cleared his throat.

'The storm's one reason,' he said.

There was a twinkle in the big man's eye as he walked towards them. 'And the other,' he said, 'probably has something to do with those riders we can all hear approaching the town in considerable haste.'

Rafe's jaw tightened. He swung around, saw the consternation in Seth's face as he cast a glance towards the open double doors — then swung around yet again when the stranger stepped close to him and spoke quickly and urgently.

'You're brothers — am I right?'

'How d'you know — ?'

'Resemblance. There's no mistaking it. Your names are . . . ?'

'Now hold on a minute — '

'I can help you get out of here with your hides intact, but I'd like to know who you are — that's reasonable, isn't it?'

Cautious hope surged within Rafe. Hadn't he asked Seth if he believed in fate?

Swiftly, he said, 'I'm Rafe Laramie, that chunky fellow's my brother, Seth.'

'All right.' The big man nodded. 'Now, listen, those riders don't know you're in here, and there's no reason they should get to know. But if they do, you can still get away with this, only for it to work we've got to play this right.'

'Why — ?'

'Why me? Why am I doing this? Maybe I see kindred spirits, men I could trust . . . men I could use.'

'You know our names, but just who the hell are you?' Rafe said, his nerves jumping as the rattle of hoofs swelled to thunder as riders turned into Greybull.

With elaborate ceremony, the stranger swept his pearl-grey Stetson from his head and across his body as he bowed gracefully.

'My name's Mort Sangster,' he said. 'But most people in these parts call me King.'

And even in those desperate moments as men intent on hanging him and his brother from the nearest tree poured into town, for the life of him Rafe Laramie couldn't tell if the tall man with the mocking smile was joking, or deadly serious.

# 4

As soon as the wet, dishevelled and weary posse swung into Greybull, Marshal John Senior pulled back his horse until those behind him crowded in close and were forced to slow. Then, at that reduced pace, half-a-dozen horses moving and jostling at an untidy walk, he led the way down the broad street.

'Can't see 'em,' he said, eyes never still, speaking his thoughts out loud and not much caring who was listening. 'We know they're here, because we've been so close we were damn near treading on their hair. And they didn't shoot off to right or left of the trail, or we'd've seen 'em — correct, Charlie?'

Nudging his horse closer to the lawman the 'breed, Charlie Flower, who was the posse's tracker, grinned happily. Beneath his black moustache his teeth flashed white in the moon-light.

'*Ellos están aquí, sin duda*,' he said seriously. 'They are here, John, there is no doubt.'

'And in a town this size, there's not many places they can be hiding,' Senior said. 'But then again, I don't suppose two desperate men need much space if they aim to disappear.'

At his shoulder, a wad of chewing tobacco bulging his unshaven cheek, Tone Worthington joined in the conversation.

'Quit arguing with yourself, John. If they leave them in plain sight, their horses'll give 'em away. So it's two desperate men, two wrung-out horses, and now you put yourself in their shoes and tell me what you'd do.'

'Get 'em off the street.'

'Best place for that?'

John Senior hooked a thumb towards the yawning double doors of Greybull's livery barn. As they rode by, harness jingling, he knew each of the armed men riding behind him was gazing in that direction with understandable uneasiness. The big doors had been flung wide, held back by short ropes looped over hooks set in the building's front walls. The moonlight reached those doors, painted them with pale light, trickled through the wide opening and was smothered by the shadows. The darkness was not absolute: a single oil lamp was a pin-prick of yellow light in the depths of the barn. But any man hiding in there would be lost in the shadows; any man approaching the building would present a clear target, outlined against the comparative brightness of the moonlit street and the oil lamps on the opposite plank walk.

'Max, Eddie, you two stay here, keep watch. Position yourselves directly across the street from the barn. Anything moves in there — you know what to do.'

The two men fell away, let their horses drift to the far plank walk. Worthington nodded understanding.

'You're going to talk to George Adams?'

'Picking his brains makes good sense,' Senior said, and he smiled bleakly. 'It's his town anyway, so it's courtesy, but if I know George he'll want to be there if there's any shooting.'

'If there is any shooting here in Greybull,' Worthington said, 'it'll be the first George has heard since he pinned on that badge.'

'All the more reason for him to be hungry for a slice of the action.'

They'd reached the jail. Both men swung down. They left Charlie Flower and Donovan, the sixth member of the posse, sitting easy in the saddle as they looked back up the street, and entered the office.

The man seated behind the desk was enormous. Fully six foot six tall, carrying enough weight with it to put everything perfectly in balance, he had iron-grey hair and a moustache to match and was as brown as an Indian.

'Don't tell me,' he said, the weariness

in his voice failing to hide his intense interest. 'This is all about those two fellows who were sucked into town by the storm?'

Senior was smiling. 'Yeah, and it's good to see you again, George.'

He leaned across the desk. They shook hands. Worthington had stayed back by the door. He nodded at the Greybull marshal, then raised an eyebrow.

'You watched them ride in, but let me tell you what happened next. They promptly took themselves and their horses into the barn — am I right?'

'That's what they did. Me and my deputy, we both saw them, remarked on them somewhat casually — but now you've got me a mite concerned. First off, they were strangers seeking shelter. But if a posse's after 'em then those two ain't no angels, and Dusty Rhodes over there in the barn is too long in the tooth to outface a couple of desperate owlhoots.'

Senior nodded. 'They robbed the

56

Alamo bank. One of them murdered the chief cashier.'

'So why the hell are you in here and not in there after them?' George Adams thundered, jaw bulging.

He came out of his seat in one fluid movement and suddenly the room seemed full of the big marshal. One hand reached out and snatched a shotgun from the rack. The other swept his sweat-stained Stetson from the desk and planted it on his white thatch. Then he was stamping his way towards the door, and both Senior and Worthington were brushed aside like roadside weeds.

★   ★   ★

As soon as he heard the jail door crash open, Mort Sangster clicked softly with his tongue and began leading his palomino up the runway towards the open doors. He had emerged from the shadows into the pool of moonlight and almost reached the open air when big George Adams came charging across the street. He was flanked by two men, one of whom wore a star on his vest. All three men had their hands on their six-guns. Adams could see two men in the shadows across the street. Another two were walking their horses across from the jail.

'Where the hell are you going, Sangster?' Adams said shortly.

'Well, now, I guess I'm heading for home if nobody objects.'

'Who's in there?'

Sangster turned, and made a great show of peering into the gloom. Then he turned, wide-eyed and innocent, and smiled ingratiatingly.

'As far as I know, George, there was nobody 'cept me and old Dusty.'

'Someone else was.' This was the unknown lawman, a steely-eyed character looking tired but resolute. 'My name's John Senior. With my posse I've pursued two men from Alamo, through a violent summer storm, and now we're here. George Adams watched them enter this barn. As you were also in

58

there, you must have seen them.'

'Ah, yes,' Sangster said, smiling crookedly, 'if you mean those two drifters — '

'Two bank robbers.'

'If you say so.' Sangster shrugged. 'They wore no such labels, and I took them at face value.'

'Fair enough, but we're wasting time,' George Adams said. 'We know they were in there, and so do you — but where are they now?'

Sangster let the question hang, frowning deliberately so that it looked as if he were seriously considering the question.

'They rode out,' he said at last. 'I guess you closed your eyes for a while. They left their exhausted mounts here, took two fresh — '

'Stole two horses,' Adams said flatly. 'So now they're killers *and* horse-thieves.'

'I seem to recall they said something about bringing those mounts back when they've finished with them.'

Then all the men gathered at the barn's entrance turned as a lanky, yawning figure stepped out of the livery barn's ramshackle office.

George Adams strode to meet him.

'Just woken, Dusty?'

'Just *been* woken,' the tall old man said, hawking noisily and spitting between his stockinged feet.

'You should be grateful. According to Sangster here, two horses you had stabled have been stolen by a couple of bank robbers.'

Dusty Rhodes flashed a toothless grin.

'Could've fooled me,' he said. 'Only had but the two in there, first two stalls, and I can hear them chomping away from here.'

Adams's jaw jutted.

'Let's go see.'

Carrying the shotgun like a club, he swung on his heel and led the way into the barn. Rhodes went after him, his severe limp causing him to rock from side to side but not slowing him in the least. He was followed by the Alamo lawman, John Senior.

For the moment, Mort Sangster let them all go. He stood with his hand resting lightly on the patient palomino's warm neck. Amused because he knew exactly what the lawmen were about to discover — indeed, hadn't he hinted at what they should expect? — he looked across at John Senior's partner, nodded and winked.

'A night full of surprises,' he said, expecting no answer and getting just that. Then, turning, he looked up the street.

Thirty yards away, a man was standing in the shadows outside the Greybull Palace. He was wearing a dark suit, but his position was given away by his white shirt and the light from the saloon falling on his pale face. Sangster had spotted him as soon as he emerged from the barn to meet George Adams and the Alamo lawman. Now he glanced about him, saw he was not being observed, and nodded his head twice.

There was no acknowledgement from the mysterious onlooker. He simply moved away, and where he had been nothing remained but impenetrable shadow.

Flicking the reins over the palomino's head so it would stand, Sangster followed the other men into the barn's gloom.

Dusty Rhodes was opening the first stall. He held the gate ajar, and slipped inside. As Sangster drew closer he could hear the old hostler's exclamations of surprise, and watched with considerable delight as the two lawmen exchanged glances then pulled the stall's gate wide.

As they did so, the hostler came tumbling out.

'Dang me, that ain't the horse I put in there,' he cried.

Hastily, fumbling, he pulled open the adjoining gate and with his skinny neck jutting like a turkey-cock's he thrust his bald head into the stall. When he emerged again, his eyes were wide.

'Wrung out,' he said, arching his old back and slamming bony hands on bony hips. 'Damn fellers took two fresh thoroughbreds and left me a couple of tired nags.' He glared. 'Bank robbers, you say? *Horse-thieves*, is what I say, and if I catch 'em they'll hang for it.'

'What about saddles and saddle-bags?' Senior said.

'What about 'em?' said Rhodes, clearly believing the lawman to be deranged. 'They ain't *there*, that's what's about 'em, because when those two horse rustlers left here they were *ridin'* on those saddles, that's what they were doing.'

Talking volubly, gesturing with his long bony arms, he was already hobbling rapidly back towards the double doors. With the two lawmen following close behind him — and Sangster again taking up the rear — he limped out into the street and stood with hands on hips.

'Gone,' the old man said, looking up and down the street and shaking his head in disbelief. 'Not a sign of 'em anywhere.'

Max and Eddie, who had been posted on the other side of the street, had walked their horses over to join Charlie Flower and Donovan. Tone Worthington moved across to have a quiet word with all four men. John Senior looked hard at the Greybull marshal.

'Any ideas, George?'

Adams shook his head.

'My guess is they're making for the hills — but that could be east or west. On the other hand, they could be heading north or south, so unless King Sangster's got something to tell us — '

'Is he saying you saw what was going on?' Dusty Rhodes yelped, swinging on Sangster and causing him to step back in alarm. 'Hell fire, that just about explains everything, wouldn't surprise me if you knew what was going on *before* those fellers rode into town.'

'Whoa, now,' Sangster said. 'Your words and tone of voice are highly offensive, old man.'

'Offensive be damned,' Rhodes said, his voice dripping contempt. 'Listen, Sangster, these youngsters wearing shiny lawmen's badges may be fooled, but I've got your measure. You're a bad 'un. Ever since you started hangin' around Greybull I've been watchin' you, waitin' for you to make a move. I think that time's come. You're up to no good, Sangster. I've a hunch you and those two bank-robbing horse thieves are in it together — up to your necks.'

# 5

In the cool sweet darkness of the loft that ran the length of the livery barn, Rafe and Seth Laramie had sat and waited. They'd listened to the jail doors crash open, followed in their minds the progress of the lawmen as they ran across the street to the barn, then hung on to every word that was said down below. They'd heard the town marshal, and the leader of the posse that had been harrying them for hours; they'd noted what had been said by Sangster — who'd said he was known as King but had not once been so called — and the unseen hostler who had come tumbling out of his office to rant and rave at his loss and everybody else's stupidity.

Eyes closed, sitting alongside their rigs and with their backs to the dusty timber wall with their arms hugging

66

their knees, they'd waited and sweated.

Now, Rafe turned to look at Seth.

'Gone. All of 'em,' he said quietly. 'The marshal back to the jail. The others, the Alamo boys? — well, I guess the saloon's where they'll freshen up. They'll drown their sorrows, figure out what to do next. Sangster's idea worked. They believe we rode out. Now they're flummoxed.'

'Not for long.'

'Why?'

'Because we didn't ride out,' Seth said, 'and those two thoroughbred horses we stole ain't stolen. All we did was move 'em to the end stalls, replace them with our spent mounts. That old hostler was fooled because he'd just woke up and he was rattled, and the rest were carried along by his anger. But that's all over, and the old boy's had time to think. I can hear him brewing coffee down below. Next thing is he'll wander out, those thorough-breds in the end stalls will attract his attention — and it'll be all over for us.'

'Maybe we'd've been better off leaving saddles and saddle-bags with the horses. That way it would have been clear to the man leading the posse that we're carrying no bank money, and so are not the men they're after.'

'Except they would quickly have figured out we'd stashed that money somewhere,' Seth said, smiling ruefully.

Rafe sighed reluctant agreement, dragged out the makings and flicked open a cigarette paper — then felt the pressure of Seth's hand on his arm and replaced tobacco and papers in his vest pocket with a grimace of frustration.

'You're right. If I don't set fire to the dry straw and burn us alive, that old-timer down there will smell the smoke and then it *will* be all over.'

Seth was grinning at his brother's lapse. Then he sobered, and said, 'What d'you make of that feller Sangster?'

'Because of him, we're still free.'

'And he's given us directions to his place, told us we're welcome there.'

'Then again,' Rafe pointed out, 'that

old hostler wasn't exactly testifying to Sangster's honesty and integrity.'

'But should that concern us? Right now we're bank robbers, killers and horse-thieves. We're in no position to point fingers, and we need all the help we can get.'

'To do what?'

For a moment Seth was silent. Rafe knew his younger brother was pondering before answering. They had always thought alike, their minds moving along parallel trails, and he would at once have understood what Rafe was getting at. He would understand that Rafe was concerned with the long-term implication of what had happened. Getting away from the posse was one thing, and Sangster's help had got them halfway there; clearing their names was likely to prove much more difficult.

'On the other hand,' Seth said, as if Rafe had spoken aloud, 'that posse doesn't *know* our names. If they don't know our names, finding us at some time in the future could prove difficult.'

'Doesn't alter the fact that we'll never feel safe.' Rafe rolled sideways, and swung nimbly to his feet. 'The only way I'm going to feel secure is if we bring those bank robbers to justice.'

'And finding them could prove as difficult for us as finding us could be for them — the posse, that is.'

Rafe blinked. 'Say that again.'

Seth grinned. 'You heard me.' He cocked his head. 'And, come to think of it, I know that look. What have you come up with?'

Rafe, pacing stealthily with his head ducked to avoid the low beams, shook his head.

'Might be nothing.'

'But could be important. Come on, spill it.'

'Remember I told you the posse had left two men on the east bank, that they were trying to get ahead of us?'

'Vaguely. Wasn't that just after we'd crossed the Bighorn?'

Rafe nodded. 'Yes — but the idea no longer makes sense. Those boys chasing us rode into Greybull as a bunch. They're down there now — there's no more than half-a-dozen of them, and no talk of others.'

'So . . . what are you saying?'

'The weather's been a pig. The only men out in it, riding hard and fast, were those chasing or being chased. I'm beginning to think those two men I saw were the bank robbers. They'd headed south to draw the posse after them, with the intention of giving them the slip then doubling back.'

'Christ!' Seth said softly. 'And they didn't need to give the posse the slip, because we drew it away.' He leaned his head back against the timber wall, looked up at his brother. 'Has this been brought on by what that old-timer said?'

Rafe stared. 'What was that?'

'He went at Sangster like a spitting polecat. Said he'd a hunch Sangster and those two bank robbers're in it together — whatever the hell it is they're supposed to be in.'

71

'There you are, you see,' Rafe said thoughtfully. 'That part of what went on down there had completely slipped my mind, but now you've brought it up it does give us a slender lead: it's possible those bank robbers are at Sangster's place.'

'A fragile lead; we'd be going on the say-so of an old wrangler who was mad enough to say just about anything when he thought two bank robbers had stolen a couple of prize horses.' Seth pulled a face. 'Nevertheless, there could be something in it. I can't see any harm in taking up Sangster's invitation and heading on out to his place.'

'Mm — if we can.'

'On the other hand, you know my feelings on the matter. We didn't rob the Alamo bank, so why not leave well alone? Let's get the hell out of here, leave Sangster and those bank robbers — if they are in cahoots — to do what they will where they will.'

'I don't do things that way.'

'I know. You never did. When we were

kids, if something was wrong you wouldn't rest until it was put right. But this is different, Rafe. We spent four years at war, another two believing we were footloose and fancy free when in reality we were wasting our lives. So now we're on the way home — damn near there — so let's slip away from here under cover of darkness.'

Rafe had stopped pacing. Clearly not listening, he was standing chewing his lip.

'The way I see it,' he said, 'the best chance we have of getting to Sangster's place is by moving fast. You rightly pointed out that old-timer's not going to be fooled for long. Every minute we remain here takes us a minute closer to discovery.'

'I don't trust Sangster.'

Rafe dismissed the remark with a sweep of the hand. 'You also said we're in no position to point the finger. We'll look the man in the eye when we get to his place, gain his confidence, take it from there. We're heading for Sangster's place because nothing's changed and I'm still giving the orders.'

'Jesus Christ,' Seth whispered fiercely, glaring — and for an instant as he sprang to his feet he looked ready to begin swinging punches. Then, clenching his fists and glowering, he bent, swung his rig onto his shoulder and headed for the hatch.

Conscious of the energy pulsating like an electric charge within his young brother's muscular frame, Rafe grabbed his own saddle and crowded close. One false move, he knew, and they were finished — and, in his present mood, Seth was well capable of acting foolishly, and without thought.

The hatch was nothing more than a square opening in the loft's floor, the way down to the runway a wide ladder. Seth turned, and clambered down backwards. He was recklessly leaning out from the ladder, clinging to his saddle with one hand and the wide wooden rungs with the other. There was a half-smile on his face. He was looking up mockingly at Rafe.

Rafe waited until Seth had stepped onto the barn's packed earth floor, then followed him down. For a few moments they stood silently in the gloom, scarcely breathing. The same lamp was burning, but it was running low on oil. The wick was burning yellow. There was a strong smell of hot oil, and it was disturbing the horses: the two thoroughbreds Rafe and Seth had moved to the furthest stalls, and their own mounts, were stamping restlessly.

Another brighter light showed in the hostler's cubbyhole. The moon was waning; little could be seen of the street, and in any case their line of sight was restricted.

Rafe took a deep breath.

'You ready for this?'

'Ready, but not happy. I still say — '

'Forget it. We go see Sangster. Find out what he's up to. Find out if those two bank robbers are there, or if we really are paying too much attention to an old-timer's rambling.'

Rafe was moving as he spoke. Together they crept stealthily to the stalls, eased the doors open and walked out their horses. Softly, softly always with one eye on the hostler's quarters, they saddled up. Then, like wraiths preparing for a ride of phantoms, they swung weightlessly into the saddle.

'What we do,' Rafe said softly, 'is we ease out into the street, turn down towards the river and take it at a walk until we're clear of town. Up against the buildings. In shadow.'

'And if we're challenged?' Seth said.

'Go like hell, every man for himself.'

'Spoken like a hero,' Seth said, and in the gloom he and Rafe grinned like excited schoolchildren.

'Come on, feller,' Rafe said, touching his horse with his heels, 'let's get the hell out of here.'

# 6

Just inside the entrance to an alley a couple of buildings down from the Greybull Palace, John Senior was sitting on a wooden crate. A Winchester repeating rifle was resting across his thighs. He was relaxed, but becoming a little impatient, a little edgy.

Senior had been sitting there for a long time. From that position — suggested to him by George Adams — he had a clear view of the livery barn. The building adjoining the alley on his left had a wide overhang that jutted out over the plank walk. That shaky canopy effectively blocked the moon's wan light. Senior, in deep shadow, was able to keep watch with impunity.

George Adams was sitting in the alley diagonally across the street, on the far side of the livery barn. The long watch had been his idea. When John Senior had been all for heading out at once after the two bank robbers — mounted now on thoroughbred horses — George had been more cagey.

'What if,' he'd said, 'that jiggery pokery with the horses was done to fool us? What if,' he'd further suggested, 'those two varmints are still in the barn? Do we go in after them, with them holding all the cards — or do we sit outside and wait with infinite patience until they believe the coast's clear, and show themselves?'

The infinite patience bit had appealed to John Senior, who had, after all, spent a large part of the day engaged on a futile chase in atrocious weather. The idea of chasing a couple of ghosts across moonlit Wyoming held no appeal whatsoever, nor did the prospect of entering a dark barn where two armed bank robbers could be lying in wait.

Adams's plan had been adopted.

From time to time, as they waited with that infinite patience that was now coming under severe strain, Senior had seen the Greybull lawman's cigarette glowing in the darkness. He had, on those occasions, felt something close to affection for the big man. All right, kinship was perhaps closer to the mark, but it came down to the same thing: unselfishly, Adams had put himself out. A fellow officer was in need of assistance and, without a second thought, George Adams had settled down to spending what looked like being a full night without sleep — and with no perceivable gain.

Of course, Tone Worthington would take a more cynical view, Senior acknowledged. He would say that George Adams was in it for the glory — and he could well be right. The point was, Adams was there on watch while John Senior had insisted that the rest of the posse get a good night's sleep. Two bank robbers, two lawmen sitting in ambush. The odds seemed favourable, and if the bank robbers were long gone, well, no sense keeping the others —

Dammit, what was that!

Swiftly, Senior slid from the crate, dropped behind it and brought his rifle around to bear on the street.

A man on horseback had emerged from the livery barn. As Senior waited, carefully working the rifle's breech, a second rider appeared out of the gloom. Both riders stopped there and held the horses steady in the wide opening. They turned in the saddle, looking up and down the street. Then, as if satisfied, they exchanged glances and the bigger of the two men nodded. They eased their mounts away from the barn, and began walking them up the street.

It was at that moment, with his first clear view of the men he'd been chasing, that John Senior experienced a sudden twinge of uneasiness. He was given no time to consider it.

'Hold it right there,' a voice roared.

George Adams, ever watchful, had sprung into action.

From behind the crate, Senior saw the big Greybull marshal step out of the alley. Adams had abandoned his shot-gun. He had his six-gun out and levelled. He was standing with legs braced. The image presented was powerful, and could have been intimidating. But he was a full thirty yards away from the two bank robbers. At that range, in that poor light, his six-gun was an unreliable weapon — and he was facing two desperate men.

Even as his words rang out, both men spun their horses. They turned them on a dime, then raked them with spurs and drove them hard and fast back into the barn.

Adams got off two fast shots. John Senior saw the bullets gouge splinters from the doors. The single shot he managed from his Winchester splintered woodwork over the big bank-robber's head. Then once again the street was empty, the sound of gunfire nothing more than a ringing in the ears.

Senior stood up. The stink of gunsmoke was in his nostrils. His eyes were on the yawning opening that was the entrance to the livery barn. Now, they knew for certain the two bank robbers were in there, armed and dangerous.

He stepped out into the street, lifted a cautionary hand to George Adams. There was a sudden clatter. From the front door of the rooming-house opposite the Greybull Palace, Tone Worthington came tumbling. He was in pants and under-shirt, his eyes darting everywhere as he brandished a six-gun. He was closely followed by the other members of the posse: the 'breed, Charlie Flowers, carrying a shotgun, then Max, Eddie and Donovan.

They came running up as Senior started across the street. He quickly told them what all the fuss was about, then ordered them to take up positions well back on the far plank walk.

'Spread out,' he said crisply. 'Keep your eyes open, your weapons ready, but do nothing until you get the order.'

Then he left them and hurried to join George Adams.

'Got 'em, John,' Adams said. 'Worst thing they could've done was go back in there . . .'

He was still talking, but his remaining words were lost as he charged towards the livery barn. He flung himself at the nearest of the open doors, slipped the holding rope free and began to swing the huge timber panel closed. It scraped across the uneven ground. Tone Worthington ran across to help. Together they pushed the big door so that the opening was half closed.

They'd just got it in place and were running towards the second door when a rifle opened up from inside the barn. Bullets punched through the door they'd just closed. White splinters flew. Hot lead flew across the street. On the far plank walk, a man groaned softly and sank to his knees.

'You two in there, cut that out!' John Senior roared. 'We're locking you in. Then it's a question of how long it takes you to see sense. You want burning out, we'll set fire to the place.

You prefer starvation — well, you know we can sit out here until Christmas if need be. It's up to you.'

'You've got the wrong men trapped.'

Senior glanced across at George Adams. He and Worthington were manhandling the second big door across the opening. At the sound of the voice hollering from inside the barn, they stopped.

Senior nodded. 'Leave it half open.'

'They're stalling,' Adams said bluntly.

'I want to hear what he has to say.'

'He'll keep you talking while the other kicks a hole in the back wall.'

'Maybe — but I've got a feeling there's something not right.'

Careful to stay out of the line of fire, Senior moved closer to the barn.

'Who is that?'

'My name's Rafe Laramie.'

'Mine's John Senior. I'm Marshal of Alamo. Come on out, Rafe, you and your partner.'

'My brother, Seth.'

'Fine. Come on out, both of you, bring your horses and the saddle-bags containing the bank's money.'

'There is no money.'

'What did you do, stash it along the way?'

'We came over the Powder River Pass last night, crossed the Nowood and realized we were heading in the wrong direction. This afternoon we were putting that right when you saw us making the second crossing and came after us with your posse.'

'Why did you run?'

The laugh from the barn was cynical, and untroubled, and somehow that added to Senior's uneasiness.

'Reverse the roles, John,' the man called Rafe said, 'then truthfully answer your own question.'

While Senior pondered on the stark reality in that suggestion and considered his next move, there was a flurry of activity. George Adams left Worthington holding the big door and jogged across the street. Senior heard the big lawman's deep voice. Then two members of his posse leaped down from the plank walk. They ran across the street and disappeared into the alleys on either side of the livery barn.

The man struck by the stray bullet had been made comfortable against the wall of the building. The last member of the posse remained with him. George Adams clapped him on the shoulder, then leaped down into the street and rejoined Senior.

'The back of the barn's secure. That's something you should have thought of instead of wasting time jawing — '

'Senior?'

The voice from the barn again. Adams flung up his arms in exasperation.

'I'm still thinking,' Senior called, and even as the truth in what he had said hit home he was looking across at Tone Worthington and waving him over.

'Then think on this,' Rafe Laramie said. 'Me and my brother, we've survived battle conditions that make this night's business . . . '

He went on talking. Senior blanked

out the flow of words, and turned as Tone Worthington approached.

'You were one of those who saw the bank robbers doing their bloody work,' he said bluntly. 'You watched them come tumbling out of the bank, saw them mount up and ride out of Alamo. So tell me — what were they wearing?'

Worthington grimaced, narrowed his eyes.

'Dust-stained hats. Shirts, pants, boots. Nothing out of the ordinary, nothing you wouldn't see on a working cowboy.'

'Not cavalry jackets? Confederate Army?'

'No, sir,' Worthington said emphatically. 'I served in the army of the Confederacy. Something like that, I'd've spotted it at once.'

Senior pulled a face.

'You hear that, George?'

Adams nodded. There was a look of disbelief on his face.

'Are you telling me these are the wrong men? You saying you've spent most of a day and half a night chasing some fellers who had nothing to do with that bank robbery?'

Senior nodded.

'Yes, George,' he said, 'that's *exactly* what I'm saying.'

# 7

The hour after midnight. In George Adams's office, four tired men sat drinking hot coffee. Adams was behind his desk, a huge, brooding figure with a tin cup clasped in both hands. John Senior was sitting to one side. On frail chairs in the area in front of the desk, the two men wearing Confederate Army jackets looked like saddle-tramps who'd drifted into town after weeks lost in the Bighorn Mountains. Rafe Laramie didn't know whether to laugh or cry. Seth was in his usual cantankerous mood, but didn't quite know at whom to direct his venom.

'I sent the men home,' Senior told Adams. 'There was no sense a posse staying here when the men we're hunting could be halfway to Montana.'

'What about the feller with a slug in his shoulder?'

'Him too.' Senior glanced across at Rafe Laramie. 'Which one of you opened up with the rifle?'

'That was my brother,' Rafe said. 'If it had been me, you'd have had more than one man down, and they'd've stayed down.'

Seth rolled his eyes. 'I never yet knew an officer who could hit a barn door from the inside — '

'That's pretty well all you *did* hit — '

'Cut it out,' George Adams snarled. 'This is my office, my jail, and I'm big enough to throw both of you in the cells for a night. Would do, too, if John hadn't got ideas for you.'

Rafe stared. 'What ideas? We already told you we've been heading home for the best part of two years.'

'Then another couple of days here won't bother you,' Senior said easily.

'Doing what?'

'It was Mort Sangster's idea to move the horses about in the barn — right?'

'He decided to help us out, yes — but so what?'

'Bank robberies have a way of taking hard cash away from the men who earned it,' George Adams said, cutting in. 'For example, those horses you moved were high-stepping thoroughbreds. They belong to a crotchety old-timer who's been ranching out the Shoshone River way for half a century. He's too far away to bank in Alamo, so he's lost nothing yet, but if those outlaws move fast and choose another town to hit — it could be Lovell or Cowley to the north of here — I know Joe Corrigan uses one or both of those banks. So . . .'

'King Sangster said — '

'King?' Adams rolled his eyes. 'Don't make me laugh, feller. That's a sobriquet he chose for himself, and nobody I know of takes one damn bit of notice.'

'That's what I figured, but, whoever he is, he told us he recognized kindred spirits,' Seth said. 'He also said he could use us, and now you seem to be saying the same thing.' He grinned across at Rafe. 'What is it about us, big Brother, that's suddenly got people falling over themselves to enlist our help?'

'Could be those army jackets you're wearing,' Senior said quietly. 'The suggestion of authority, the familiarity with discipline; the ability to recognize nonsense when you hear it. The point is, by helping Sangster — or appearing to do so — you would be helping George, and you'd be helping me.'

There was a moment's silence. Then Rafe grimaced.

'Seems to me you're another man who puts too much store in what's been said by an old hostler.'

'That may be true,' Senior said, 'but if there's a possibility he's even half right about Sangster, surely we should look into it?'

'Mort Sangster,' George Adams said, throwing in his nickel's worth, 'is a rascal. I for one am willing to trust Rhodes's instincts — but I think linking Sangster to those bank robbers may be a step too far.'

'I tend to agree. The only reason

Rhodes linked Sangster to those bank robbers is because he believed he'd helped them — meaning us — get away,' Rafe said. 'But the bank robbers were never in his barn, or anywhere near it, so that supposed link never existed. However — '

'However,' Seth interrupted, 'you're pretty sure you saw those two bank robbers on the other side of the river, heading in this direction. And as we know Sangster's got a place in the hills — '

'Top end of a box canyon,' Adams said, nodding. 'It cuts a gash in the side of the mountains.'

There was a short silence, eventually broken by Senior.

He said, 'Right now we're clutching at straws. Rafe, you say you sighted those two men. That's news to me, but I do know George here believes Mort Sangster's up to no good. Put those facts together and at least we've got something to go on, a thread we can hang on to.'

Adams nodded agreement. 'We can also make it all nice and legal, if that's what's bothering you. I'll swear you two fellers in as deputies, here and now. You can spend what's left of the night in the cells, and be heading for Sangster's place soon's the sun's up.'

'If it's any help,' John Senior said, 'I'll ride with you.'

Seth was shaking his head. 'You're welcome to do so, but whether you do or you don't means nothing to Rafe. The decision to ride to Sangster's place was settled long before we came down from the loft. The only thing that's changed is the reason behind it, and my big brother doesn't pay too much attention to why he does things.'

'In that case, come with me,' George Adams said, climbing to his feet. 'I'll dig up a couple of badges, swear you in, then show you to a couple of cornhusk mattresses in those nice clean cells I was talking about.'

# 8

Mort Sangster's route away from Greybull took him across the Bighorn River and in a north-easterly direction towards Hunt Mountain and the foothills of the Bighorns. He rode while the moon was still floating high in clear skies, making the river crossing with difficulty as the storm's run-off tumbling down from the high slopes turned usually placid waters into raging rapids.

After some five miles he knew he was following the trail taken earlier by Lake Rafferty and Milo Crane. The two outlaws had always planned to head south after the bank robbery in Alamo, then cross the Nowood and double back when they were clear of the inevitable pursuit. Rafe and Seth Laramie appearing out of nowhere to draw the posse away would have been an unexpected bonus. Sangster could imagine the two ruffians crowing with laughter as they headed north with saddle-bags stuffed with money.

For a while as he rode, Sangster pondered nervously on the outcome of the bank robbery. There was no guarantee that it had been successful; a posse would have been raised even if Rafferty and Crane had fled empty handed. But, knowing how closely Kieran Stark was watching the Alamo bank robbery, Sangster blanked his mind to the possibility of failure. The man's wrath was awesome to behold when he was crossed. If Rafferty and Crane had failed, no man caught in the same room as the Greybull business-man would consider himself safe.

Sangster shivered at the thought.

The sheer blue funk that caught hold of him caused him to push his horse too hard. By the time he turned east into the familiar box canyon and his horse's hoofs were thudding on grass carpeting the slopes, the animal was blowing through flared nostrils. White foam was flying from its flanks, and several times it stumbled, almost going down.

Jaw clenched, Sangster cursed its ornery hide and held it upright by will power and the strength of his arms. He rode now mostly in the shadow of thickly wooded slopes, craning his head impatiently to see around the next bend, willing the cabin to appear, praying for the sight of two horses in the small corral — yet knowing that their presence would prove nothing.

Fear remained to haunt him. As he rode onwards, a thin film of sweat was cold on his brow. He rode for another half-mile. That distance, always through trees now close enough to pluck at his clothing, had stretched to a full mile before, abruptly, he came out of the forest and onto the edge of a moonlit clearing. There, for a few minutes, he reined in the exhausted horse and contemplated the unusual location that always left him with a feeling of awe.

He was holding the horse on the edge

of an area of open land formed where the canyon widened and the slopes on either side, rocky and precipitous, were denuded of all vegetation. Any stranger emerging from the trees and gazing at what lay before him would at once assume that he could go no further: he would believe he had reached the end of the box canyon, and would reluctantly turn his horse and retrace his steps.

Morton Sangster knew different. And once, in the Greybull Palace, when too much whiskey had passed his lips, he had mentioned that knowledge to Kieran Stark.

Shaking his head, his lips tight, Sangster spoke to his exhausted horse and rode out of the trees and across the stretch of open grass that led up to the cabin. Lamplight gleamed in the single window. As Sangster drew closer he saw the two horses in the makeshift corral — and the iron band that had been restricting his breathing very slightly slackened its grip. He swung down at the peeled-pine hitch rail. Loose-tied his horse. Turned once to look back the way he had come and marvel yet again at how one man standing where he was now would control the approaches.

Then he clattered up the creaking wooden steps and pounded across the gallery. At his fierce push the door swung open with a groan. Two men sitting at a crude pine table looked up impassively as he crashed across the threshold.

Sangster stood, gasping. He looked at Lake Rafferty, and Milo Crane. He took a deep breath, and dashed a hand across his damp face.

'Well?' he said.

'Relax,' Lake Rafferty said. 'We got it. Could be as much as five thousand bucks. Your troubles are over.'

★　★　★

'You've got no idea the troubles I've got,' Sangster said. 'What you did is a start. The prelude to greater achievements. But don't talk to me about troubles being over.'

Ten minutes had raced by. Sangster was sitting by the iron stove that glowed cherry-red. A tin cup was held in one hand. It had been full of whiskey, but was now almost empty. There was a flush on his face, emphasized by his crown of crisp white hair. His eyes were already glassy.

'Rafferty plugged a bank clerk,' Crane said. 'Does that count as piling trouble upon trouble?'

'Who you plugged is your problem,' Sangster said. 'I'm a couple of steps removed from that robbery. If anything goes wrong, you're on your own, so you'd better make sure that doesn't happen.'

He let that sink in, then gestured towards the two saddle-bags that had been tossed carelessly against the cabin wall.

'What I want you to do now is empty those onto the table. Then we'll do an accurate count.'

Rafferty winked at Crane. 'Good job we took a slice off the top before we got here.'

'For your own good,' Sangster said, 'I'll forget you said that.'

Rafferty, leaning back as he poured whiskey into a cup, was wide-eyed and innocent.

'Come on, Mort, you don't seriously think we'd milk a few bucks then tell you about it?'

'Wrong. Working a double bluff would come as second nature to you. And after what happened, hell, you probably think your luck's in.' Sangster stared speculatively at the two outlaws, and cocked an eyebrow. 'You did see those two fellows who came down from the hills and pulled the pursuit away from you?'

'Sure. Watched 'em cross the river with bullets whistling by their ears.'

'Well, I can tell you now they made it to Greybull minutes ahead of the posse.'

'And then what? Got cornered? Gunned down? Strung up from the nearest tree?'

'I don't know. They were still on the loose when I left town. My guess is they're crafty enough to stay one jump ahead of the law,' Sangster said, not mentioning how he'd stepped in to help the Laramie brothers, still not sure why he had. Because they were brothers, and he felt a certain affinity? Because Stark's plans called for more men, of a certain special kind? Well, that was reason enough — but why should he do Stark's work for him? Why, for God's sake, after all these years, had he ever got involved with the man?

Well, he thought, one good reason could be because I foolishly let slip about this place — that's why.

Rafferty was shrugging. 'Let them get clear away. They've done their bit for us. And if Stark was in town he'll have seen what's going on and know we made it.'

'He was there, and saw everything, so

let's get those bags emptied — '

Sangster broke off. An icy chill broke through the dullness caused by strong whiskey. He looked narrow-eyed at the two outlaws, saw that neither of them had heard anything out of the ordinary. So, he'd been mistaken; he had not heard the hoofbeats of a solitary horse approaching the cabin. But it would happen, it had been planned that way. The minutes were fast ticking away, and when that solitary rider emerged from the trees and began crossing the clearing, then he wanted these two men long gone. Not because he didn't want them caught in the cabin, but because if they were still there when that rider arrived, they would know too much for their own good. There was an old saying, something about a little learning being dangerous. Change that dangerous to fatal, and that just about summed up the hypothetical but entirely possible situation.

Over the rim of the tin cup Rafferty was watching him with amusement.

'Getting nervous? Hearing the thundering hoofs of ghostly posses, Sangster?'

'If he is,' Crane said, 'we've got something here that's going to banish those cold chills, warm him up a treat.'

He was up on his feet. He dragged the two heavy saddle-bags across the dirt floor, unbuckled the straps and upended the bags over the table. The contents spilled out. Bundles of banknotes formed a heap. The heap became too large for the table top. Loose notes, and packets secured by rubber bands, slid over the edge and flopped or floated to the floor. Several rubber-banded packets landed in Rafferty's lap. He dropped his free hand onto them, grinned wolfishly at Crane.

Sangster stared at the money, on the table, on the floor, and ran his tongue along his lips.

'And now,' he said hoarsely, 'you two can go.'

'What about the count?' Crane said, still holding the empty bags.

'I'll do it.'

'Yeah, and the pay for the boys who did the dirty work?'

'You'll get it. But I want you out of here.'

Rafferty put the empty cup down with excessive care.

'Talking of pay, what say I keep hold of what was dumped in my lap, and we call it quits?'

For a moment Sangster hesitated. Then, his nerves quivering as his ears listened for the approaching hoofbeats, he nodded quickly.

'It's a deal. Now, you know where you're going?'

'Jesus Christ,' Rafferty said disgustedly as he climbed to his feet, spilling more money from the table as he did so.

'All right, all right. Take the bags, take that cash that conveniently fell into your lap, and when you get where you're going, stay put. By tomorrow, you'll have company.'

'Company?'

'Fellows like yourselves. Owlhoots.

Renegades.' Sangster shrugged.

'A regular nest of rattlers,' Crane said, grinning.

'A band of *irregulars*,' Rafferty said, and he waited until Crane had swung the saddle-bags over his shoulder then followed him through the door.

It slammed behind the two bank robbers.

Sangster stood stock still, in an attitude of listening. He listened to the hollow thump of boots on the gallery; the jingle of bridles; the sound of the horses moving away. And still he stayed motionless. He remained in that position until, several minutes later, another sound reached his ears. When he heard it, faint beads of sweat broke out on his brow and he drew a deep, shuddering breath.

When the door at last groaned open, Sangster was down on his knees with crumpled greenbacks clutched in both hands. He sat back on his heels, aware that cold sweat was now trickling down his face. With a forced, sickly grin, he held up his hands and let the money crackle in his fists.

'Isn't that the sweetest thing you ever saw or heard, Kieran?'

The tall, thin man in the dark suit let his pale eyes take in the man on the floor, and the table heaped with stolen money.

'It's a start,' Kieran Stark said. 'I call that the taster that whets our appetites. After this, we can get down to the serious business of making our fortunes.'

★ ★ ★

'Did you stay in town long enough to see how that posse got on?'

Stark had removed his jacket. He had been stuffing the money back into the saddle-bags. His shirt was damp at the armpits, his face pink, and at his hairline a thin line of sweat glistened. He straightened his back and dropped into one of the chairs.

'Long enough to hear Rhodes accusing you of being in cahoots with those two bank robbers. Who, as we both know,' Stark said with an evil grin, 'had nothing at all to do with the Alamo bank robbery.'

'Yes, their sudden appearance was a stroke of luck,' Sangster said.

He wondered briefly if he should tell Stark of his part in the confrontation in Greybull, and knew at once that he should do so without delay. Stark would find out sooner or later and his wrath, when he was crossed or deceived, could be wondrous to behold. Sangster shivered, and smiled weakly as he caught Stark looking at him.

'When offered a gift, take it, that's what I say,' he began, turning his back and busying himself at the stove.

'If you're talking about Rafferty and Crane, well, yes, of course they did.'

The coffee-pot clattered on the hot iron as Sangster almost dropped it.

'I was talking about us. About you and me, and those fellows' involvement in your grand scheme.'

The coffee pot was in place, and

beginning to hiss. He turned around, rammed his hands into his pockets. Stark was staring at him, his eyes hard.

'They ceased to be associated with us when they drew the posse away from Rafferty and Crane. Their next association will be with the hangman.'

Sangster shook his head.

'They won't be caught. I told them how to give those lawmen the slip. Told them, when they'd done so and were clear, they'd be welcome here because I could use them.'

The hissing coffee-pot was suddenly loud in the silence. The silence went on and on. Then Stark stirred himself.

'Up to now,' he said quietly, almost as if he were talking to himself, 'robberies of any kind have been committed by outlaws who have always been of low intelligence. There has been little planning. What planning there has been, has been limited, rudimentary. So either the robberies have failed, or the robbers themselves have very soon been caught.'

'I know — '

'I will change all that,' Stark went on. 'In an entirely new approach to crime, robberies will still be committed by men who are one step up the ladder from beasts of the field, but the planning will be done by me — and, as I am an intelligent, reputable business-man, I will be above suspicion.'

'We need men who — '

'We've got men,' Stark said harshly. 'Yesterday, two men proved their worth; they are unintelligent, but capable. Another four of that same kind will very soon be joining them. All of their adult lives those men have operated on the wrong side of the law. Why do you talk about need? Why do we need two men you know nothing about, two men who could *ruin* my plans?'

'Their name's are Rafe and Seth Laramie. I need them because of their military experience. Their experience will be the link between you and those men you clearly despise. And the Laramie brothers will do exactly as I say because of . . . because of the hold I have over them.'

Sangster swallowed, because he saw the sudden change in Stark's expression; the swift understanding; the instant, familiar contempt.

'What hold would that be?'

'The law believes them to be bank robbers. Their fate is in my hands.'

'They could ride away at any time, disappear into the night.'

'And always be hunted. Always looking over their shoulder.'

Stark nodded. His eyes were amused.

'Is that why *you* stay?'

'You know why I stay,' Sangster said hoarsely.

'Do I? What I know is that you murdered my father, and my mother, left me to rot in an orphanage — '

'*My* father, *my* mother — and I've always denied that accusation, vehemently, vociferously.'

'But to no avail,' Stark said curtly. 'You're my brother, but I don't believe you. You slit their throats, and to this day I don't know why.'

'And you never will know why, because that killing was done by renegades. I was fourteen years old, for God's sake. You think I could slit *anyone's* throat, never mind murder my own parents?'

'Blunt answer: yes, I do.'

Sangster clamped his jaw shut. He turned away and, with a shaking hand, poured two cups of coffee. He carried one to the table, placed it in front of Stark.

'Renegades raided the homestead,' he said in a voice devoid of emotion. 'I heard the noise, pulled the blankets over my head because noise of some kind was nothing unusual. But then I heard horses, moving away — several horses. I went to investigate. You know what I found, because that same night-mare scene confronted you when you awoke.'

'I found two dead bodies, covered in blood. I was six years old,' Stark said, 'and my brave brother had run away.'

'All right.' Sangster nodded. 'When you found me, last year, rode into Greybull and confronted me, I admitted that crime: I deserted my young brother. But I also told you that the death of my parents was a release. They mistreated me, always: for years I had been their unpaid slave.' He laughed. 'If I'd been really brave, I would have left home as soon as I was able to ride, but I stayed on.'

'When you murdered our parents, and ran,' Stark said, 'the mistreatment you say you endured came to me. I moved from orphanage to orphanage, foster parent to foster parent, all of them cruel, and none worse than those who gave me the name of Stark.'

'But it's over,' Sangster said wearily. 'We've moved on.'

'Moving on doesn't mean the past can be changed; moving on doesn't mean there's any forgiving. I think you're lying, and I know that if I hand you over to the law, today, tomorrow, next year — no judge or jury will believe your story. You'll hang, Mort.'

'You'd do that? You'd . . . you'd murder your own brother?'

'Oh, for God's sake, you make me sick. Drink your coffee. We both know why you've taken a shine to these Laramies: you see in them what might have been between you and me. Well, let me be blunt: settle for what you've got, because it's not going to get any better.'

The coffee cup shook in Sangster's hand.

'And the Laramie brothers?'

Stark shrugged. 'Apparently you've gone too far to backtrack. Another way of putting it is, you've stuck your neck out. Now you'd better pray to God you haven't made one hell of a big mistake.'

# PART TWO

# THE OUTLAWS

# 9

For Rafe and Seth Laramie, breakfast the next morning was fried beef, eggs and coffee partaken well before sunrise in Greybull's clean little café. The café was run by George Adams's daughter. George didn't bother rousing her or her husband, but instead donned an apron and took over the job of cook and waiter.

'Easier this way,' he explained, as he leaned back against a table — his weight causing it to creak — and watched the brothers clean their plates and sit back with satisfied sighs. 'Gets cooked and served the way I like it — which is a change from what my wife dishes up — and gives me time to get to know you boys.'

'Nothing to know beyond what's already been said,' Rafe said. 'Four years at war, another two drifting.' He grimaced. 'If I hadn't crossed a river by mistake, that posse would have gone after the real bank robbers and we'd be another fifty miles closer to home.'

'Home being?'

'Montana. A homestead in the shadow of Big Baldy. Where our pa was born, and died, and where Ma has been waiting . . . well . . . for too damned long.'

Adams looked up as the street door clattered open and John Senior walked in. The Alamo marshal was freshly shaved, but the clothes he had worn through the previous day's storm had dried stiff and wrinkled. He nodded to the three men.

'I've eaten,' he said, taking in the empty plates. 'The pretty woman who runs the rooming-house dished up a hot breakfast without being asked.'

'That sounds like Abby,' Adams commented fondly.

'Which means,' Senior went on, 'we should be ready to ride.'

'Or perhaps not,' George Adams said,

and suddenly all eyes were on the big Greybull marshal.

'It might look as if I run this town, and in many ways I do, but other men have influence, and I'm forced to listen to them. In Wyoming cattle country, one of those men is Kieran Stark. He rode in this morning before you boys had crawled out of bed, wants to know what's going on.'

Rafe frowned. 'Rode in from where?'

'He has a small place a mile or so out of town.'

'What can he hope to get from us?'

'Not a lot,' Adams said. 'We know it, and deep down he does too. But Stark heads the Wyoming Cattlemen's Association.' He shook his head. 'His position is questionable, balanced on a knife edge. Word is he secured the appointment by lying through his teeth. Gave himself an impressive record in the cattle business that doesn't hold water.'

'Frustrating for you.'

'Yeah, well. That money going missing from the Alamo bank directly affects several big ranchers.' He shrugged. 'I guess Stark wants to show he's doing his job, keeping up to date.'

'Finger on the pulse,' John Senior said, and grimaced.

'More like two hands holding the shreds of his reputation together.' Adams said that with a faint smile, then quickly became serious. 'I've mentioned nothing to Stark of what we discussed yesterday. And it seems to me that we were wrong in a couple of respects. First is that you, John, cannot ride with these boys.'

Senior was nodding. 'I've already realized that. Anyway, my day will be taken up with a ride to Alamo. I need to disband the posse officially, then get back here as fast as I can.'

'Good,' Rafe said, nodding. 'We had a discussion, me and Seth, while we were in those cells. We don't want deputizing, and if we're going after Sangster and those two bank robbers it has to be kept in the dark; we ride out of town, just the two of us, for all the world as if we're taking up our journey towards home.'

'And that's what we tell this Stark fellow,' Seth said.

'Fair enough.' Adams nodded, and stepped away from the table as he stripped off his apron. 'I told him you'd see him in the Palace. Vin Cassiday who owns the place has already opened up. Stark's waiting up there.'

Rafe and Seth left the two lawmen crossing the street to the jail, and made the short walk up to Greybull's only saloon. The street was still wet from the heavy rain, yellow pools standing in the deep wagon ruts, the dust turned to cloying mud which they tried to stamp from their boots before entering the Palace.

The big main room was gloomy, and smelt of sawdust, stale smoke and spilled liquor. A tall man was sitting at a table well away from the door, legs stretched out, a cigar smouldering in one bony hand. His dark suit was crumpled, his white shirt a little less than crisp, his boots caked. But the grey eyes were bright and intelligent and, for a reason he couldn't fathom, Rafe experienced a fleeting chill of fear when he met the man's probing gaze.

A glance at Seth told him that his brother was similarly affected. Then they'd reached the table, Stark was up on his feet, and was shaking their hands with what appeared to be genuine respect.

'I don't usually hold with men clinging to military uniforms this long after the war. Smacks too much of posturing for my liking. But George Adams has explained your situation. You've yet to make it home, and it appears that a genuine mistake by an honest lawman came close to preventing that from ever happening.'

'Lesser mortals might not have come out of that chase unharmed,' Rafe agreed. 'But we did, thank the Lord, and now we've been told you want to hear all about it.'

He pulled out a chair, straddled it,

folded his arms on the back.

'Not all. Let's say I'd like to hear your side of the story.'

'Our side's the same as their side,' Seth said, leaning back against the adjoining table. 'Like you said, an honest lawman made a mistake, but it's over now and we're heading home.'

'Which is what I'd expect you to do,' Stark said. 'However, as head of the Wyoming Cattlemen's Association it would be remiss of me not to learn all I can from the two men closest to the action. George Adams tells me you saw those bank robbers. What I'd like to know is, could you identify them?'

'No.' Rafe shook his head. 'In fact, I didn't see them, Seth did . . . ' He turned, handing over to his brother.

'They were too far away, going too fast,' Seth contributed. 'Rough-looking characters — but that's the best I can do.'

'According to John Senior, a member of his posse saw them leave the Alamo bank,' Rafe offered.

Stark nodded. 'Yes, I know, and that's where I'm heading next. It's a long ride, but worth it if it helps recover that stolen money.'

He was up out of his chair, giving them one cold, strangely calculating look before his interest in them evaporated. Five minutes after meeting him, Rafe and Seth were watching his back as he walked out of the saloon. Five minutes after that they were in the saddle and riding out of Greybull in a north-easterly direction.

★  ★  ★

The directions given to them by Morton Sangster proved easy to follow. Once across the Bighorn River they quickly found their way to the trail he had described. It took them away from the water and in the right direction, in a meandering fashion but with Hunt Mountain always visible so that they could keep a check on their course. The landscape had been washed clean by the rains. The air was cool and sweet. It was, Rafe remarked, a pleasant day to be out riding — almost too good to last.

Five miles further on, that casual remark proved to be prophetic.

'If that's the box canyon I can see up ahead,' Seth said, gazing into a distance already dancing with heat haze, 'then I think we've got company.'

'Dammit,' Rafe swore softly.

He reined in, chewing his lip, then urged his horse a few yards off the trail and up a low rise topped by trees. From there he had a clearer view ahead.

'Four of 'em,' he called. 'Look as if they've come down from the hills to the north. They would have met us head on if they'd kept going. As it is — '

He was dancing his horse back down the steep slope as he spoke, his words chopped short by the jolting descent.

' — they turned into the canyon,' Seth finished for him. 'OK, so what do we do?'

'My instinct is to keep heading for Sangster's place, but make damn sure those fellows don't spot us. They may ride on through; just because they entered the canyon doesn't mean we're all going to end up in the same place.'

'It being a box canyon,' Seth said drily, 'I'd say it was highly likely. And it makes you ponder some on Sangster's words when he said he could use us. Use us — and how many others? And for what?'

'If you're right, then maybe we should have given more credence to that old hostler's words, maybe stopped long enough to ask him a few questions. Wisdom comes with age, but I've a hunch even Rhodes is seeing only part of a much bigger picture. If we press on we could end up deep in the mire, and if you've a mind to walk away from this right now then I'm not going to argue.'

'Too late for that. The itch to find out what's going on here is beginnin' to drive me crazy.'

'Yeah, despite my misgivings — which I kept well hidden — I feel the same way,' Rafe said, grinning. 'I was grumbling for most of yesterday, but, although I hate to admit it, I can't remember having this much fun since Appomattox.'

'The Laramie brothers ride again,' Seth said, matching his grin, and with a suitably subdued whoop he lightly touched his horse with his heels and got them moving again. He led the way at a spanking pace until they turned east into the canyon. There he slowed, the two men came together, and they proceeded with circumspection.

Several times on their way up the trail that twisted between tree-covered slopes they caught fleeting glimpses of the four riders. Those men — dressed in rough clothing, bristling with weapons — were indeed watching their back trail, and only constant vigilance enabled Rafe and Seth to avoid detection. Eventually even caution was of little use to them. The trees on both sides pushed in closer, it was impossible to see more than a few yards ahead, and it was almost without warning that they broke clear of the forest and found themselves on the edge of a large clearing.

On the other side of it, as described by Mort Sangster, a cabin sat snugly against yet more thick woods backed by soaring cliffs. Pungent woodsmoke was pouring from the cabin's stone chimney stack to be flattened by an errant wind and hang like thin cloud over the clearing.

Of the four riders, there was no sign.

The unmistakable figure of Morton Sangster with his mop of white hair, buckskin jacket and fancy boots was standing on the cabin's gallery. He saw them, and lifted a hand in greeting.

'Now there's a strange thing,' Rafe said, as they acknowledged the big man's signal and set off across the open ground. 'Where do you suppose those fellows went?'

'Not ahead, that's for sure,' Seth said, 'because this is a genuine box canyon and they'd come smack up against those cliffs. I can see but one horse in that small corral — a palomino — so unless they tethered their mounts behind the cabin, it's got me beat.'

'You made it!' Sangster roared, coming to the front of the gallery and leaning stiff-armed on the rail as they reached the hitching pole and swung down.

'Making it this far was the easy bit,' Rafe said, drawing off his gloves, thrusting them into his belt and stamping up the steps. 'Now comes the hard part, and that's swallowing the tall tale I know damn well you're going to spin.'

# 10

'Can I be frank with you two boys?'

Sprawled in a chair on the gallery, a tin cup of whiskey in one hand and a cigar in the other, Rafe couldn't resist rolling his eyes in disbelief.

'If I had a cent for every time I've heard that,' he said, 'I'd be a rich man.'

'Yeah, and I'll drink to that,' Seth said — and promptly did, so deeply that his eyes watered and he was overtaken by a fit of coughing.

Mort Sangster chuckled, clearly not offended.

'Turning you two into rich men is why I invited you here, though I wasn't thinking of doing it a cent at a time. But before I go into details, I'd like to know what manner of men I'm dealing with. If, for example, you adhere to strict religious or moral codes that prevent you stepping over the line.'

'I like the way you put that,' Seth said, and he winked at Rafe. 'Tell me, Sangster, what line would that be.'

Sangster was still smiling, but suddenly his eyes were watchful.

'Depends on your point of view. Clearly, to some, it would be the line between right and wrong. To others, however — and I must confess I take this view — it's the line between rich and poor. Looked at in that way it's a line that becomes much more . . . crossable.'

'Crossable,' Rafe echoed, and he took a cautious sip of the rot-gut whiskey and felt it burn its way down his throat like molten metal. 'Tell me, Sangster, in what way do we cross it? What do we have to do?'

For a long moment Sangster seemed to be searching for a way to answer the question — perhaps, Rafe thought, for a way of doing so without putting his plans into jeopardy. Eventually he turned, and appeared to be looking at the cabin. But a moment later it became clear that his vision extended much further.

He ran fingers through his thick white hair, and a thin smile curved his lips.

'You boys, you rode up the canyon and out of the woods. You saw this cabin, backing onto yet more woods, behind those the cliffs turning the canyon into a box — that right?'

Mystified, Rafe nodded.

Remarkably swiftly for a man his age, Sangster came out of his chair.

'I'll get my horse. Tag along. There's something I want you to see.'

Not knowing what to expect, Rafe and Seth followed him out of the cabin, mounted their horses and sat facing down the slope towards the canyon mouth while Sangster saddled his palomino. But when he rode out of the corral he turned in the opposite direction, rode behind the cabin and out of their sight.

Seth looked at Rafe as they wheeled their mounts and followed the big man.

'Dammit,' he said in feigned amazement, 'I reckon he's got a gold mine in there.'

Rafe was already ahead of him, curiosity drawing him on. They had to round the corral. Once beyond that and behind the cabin, a worn trail was revealed. It entered the woods at an angle, and was immediately forced to twist and turn to skirt huge conifers that blocked the way forward. Rafe could hear Sangster a little way ahead of him, Seth close behind. The ride was short. From the dense shadow of the woods they suddenly emerged into bright sunlight. They were in a gap between woods and cliffs.

Sangster was waiting. Seated astride the palomino, one hand on the ivory butt of his pistol, he was grinning broadly.

For the canyon was not blocked. The immense rock wall was not impenetrable. Anyone venturing beyond the cabin and through the woods would discover a fissure in the rock face. Wide enough at its base for two men to ride abreast, it closed in a mere twenty feet above the canyon floor. What was formed was a tunnel with a vaulted roof. Crystal clear water tumbled through that tunnel.

'Provides me with fresh water,' Sangster said, watching them, 'but on the other side of these cliffs it does a whole lot more.'

He turned his horse and clattered into the tunnel. Rafe and Seth followed, their horses splashing through the water, the clatter of hoofs echoing from the damp stone walls. It was a ride of perhaps forty or fifty yards. When they again emerged into bright sunlight, what they saw caused them to draw rein and sit in silence.

It was broken by Sangster.

'That barrier presented by that cliff behind the cabin's an illusion, a freak of nature. Makes you think you've reached the end of a box canyon — and, in centuries gone by, that was probably true. But then something happened

— an earthquake, at the very least a geological disturbance big enough to smash solid rock and create that fissure. When it did, the way to this second valley was opened up.'

Rafe nodded. Where they had emerged the ground was on a level with the rock fissure, sloping gently upwards into the distance, and he was looking at an area probably twice the size of the large clearing leading up to Sangster's cabin. But this area was better described as a hidden valley; a place of peace and tranquillity cut off from the outside world. Through the centre of the lush meadows carpeting the valley's floor, a creek flowed — the same creek that drained through the fissure and provided water for Morton Sangster. That creek had as its source a waterfall that cascaded from the fifty-foot cliffs at the valley's eastern end. Those cliffs, Rafe realized, formed the true end of the box canyon.

'I discovered this place,' Sangster said

softly. 'And I'm going to put it to good use.'

Rafe nodded.

Across the creek, several hundred yards back from it, almost at the base of the thick woods and cliffs forming the valley's southern boundary, there were four cabins. Solidly constructed, they were now old and tumbledown, their shingle roofs sagging, their doors hanging on rotted rope or leather hinges. All around them, and especially leading down to the creek, there were signs of cultivation. But it was cultivation that had ceased untold years ago and been taken over by weeds; they were looking, Rafe surmised, at the remains of a settlement once occupied by hardy pioneers who had arrived well in advance of the current western migration.

Today, the position of those old cabins gave their new occupants a clear view in three directions, and a shield for their rear. In what looked like a new peeled-pole corral alongside the nearest cabin, Rafe counted six horses. As he watched, several men emerged from one of the cabins and stood staring towards the fissure.

'If you were wondering where those fellers we saw got to, Seth, well, now you know,' Rafe said.

'Yeah,' Seth said, 'and as we counted four and there's six horses over there, we can work out who the other two are: they robbed a bank in Alamo. From there, it doesn't take a genius to figure out what our friend here, good old Morton Sangster, has got up his sleeve.'

'You, me, and every one of us,' Sangster said. 'It's about time you understood that now you've come this far, you're in it with us — like it or not.'

★ ★ ★

They rode up the slope from the fissure and across the lush grass, then splashed through the creek and dismounted in the shade of a stand of cottonwoods. Sangster lifted a hand to the watching men, who were now sitting around a camp-fire on the banks of the creek and showed no reaction. He walked up the slope towards them. One man, tall, gangling, with weapons hanging about his bony frame like the trophies of a forgotten war, met him halfway. There was some animated talk that didn't quite carry as far as Rafe and Seth, several gestures in their direction. Then some kind of agreement was reached, and Sangster returned to perch on a boulder that was one of several scattered along the wet shingle at the creek's edge.

Rafe and Seth, feeling like prisoners running an incomprehensible gauntlet, did the same.

For a while nothing was said. Overhead the skies were darkening again, and Rafe knew that before too long the rains would return. The air was growing oppressive. The murmur of conversation drifted down to them, broken by the occasional burst of laughter. Sangster lit a cigar. Seth began whistling tunelessly through his teeth, a sure sign that he was getting edgy — which, Rafe knew, could eventually lead to explosive action.

'OK,' Rafe said at last, 'tell us what it is we've got ourselves trapped into, Sangster. Not that we need telling, of course, but I think you should spell it out.'

'Robbery,' Sangster said. 'On a grand scale.'

'With this place as what? An outlaw haven, with you directing operations, sending out bands of raiders who hit any town big enough to have a bank?'

'Banks, mail coaches.' Sangster puffed at his cigar. 'Anything holding or carrying money. But especially banks, and for a very good reason.'

'Go on, I'll bite,' Rafe said.

Sangster chuckled. 'Hitting a bank's always chancy: there's always the possibility there'll be precious little in the safe. Big risk, small return. When we begin operating, that will never happen. This is ranching country, and I know a man who can tell me when cattle's being moved, when a big herd's being sold. Better than that, he can tell me which bank the rancher uses, and the date he intends depositing cash from the sale.'

Rafe nodded slowly, digesting the information, seeing the obvious advantages.

'You know, when you led the way into that hole in the rock face,' he said, 'Seth made a remark: he reckoned you had a gold mine back here. He wasn't too far off the mark, was he? Because that's the way you see this. You believe that from here your men can ride out to hit hard and often, and never get caught. The authorities will be mystified. Banks will be robbed, and posses will see the outlaw bands responsible disappearing into thin air. They'll be left chasing shadows — that's how you see it. Am I right?'

Sangster flicked ash, nodded slowly. 'Close enough.'

Seth chuckled softly, richly, and Rafe shook his head.

'Close enough,' he echoed. 'Sure I am. I'm right because I've got your scheme all figured out. The trouble is, you're wrong, Sangster. It'll never work.'

'The Alamo bank robbery was a test. That worked.' Sangster hooked a thumb over his shoulder. 'Two of those men back there are living proof that this place is a sanctuary.'

'We made it possible by popping up in the wrong place,' Seth said. 'The Alamo posse trailed us all the way to Greybull, trapped us in the livery barn. But we were a distraction. If we hadn't led them astray they would have hunted down the real bank robbers. All the way to the canyon. All the way to your cabin.'

'And found nothing.'

'You think they'd leave it at that?' Rafe snorted. 'Come on, Sangster. They'd post a couple of guards so the canyon was secure, then commence searching. How long d'you think it'd take for them to discover the trail behind your cabin, that mighty crack in the cliff face that gives your boys an escape route into this hideaway, but also gives the game away?'

'And traps them,' Seth pointed out. 'Hell fire, one lawman with a rusty six-gun could control that hole in the wall.'

'And there's six men in here,' Sangster said softly. 'Eight, counting you two. If my boys here can't get out, it sure as hell works the other way.'

'A Mexican stand-off,' Rafe said, 'with neither side able to make any gains. But how does that help? I mean, how long could your boys hold out?'

'There's wild game in here, fish in the creek, enough water to slake an *army's* thirst, and these fellers would have all the time in the world.' Sangster shrugged. 'On the other hand, a posse's made up of working men giving up time that's precious and costing them money, lawmen with towns running wild in their absence. I'd give any posse a week at most. Then they'd begin making excuses, drifting away in ones and twos.'

Seth was on his feet, standing with hands on hips staring up at the men sitting around the camp-fire. Deliberately, he spat onto the wet shingle, then turned to face Sangster.

'We asked you to spell it out. All you've done is tell us how clever you are, how your outlaw band's going to rob banks and mail coaches using this place as a base where they cannot be touched. As an army man, I still say your strategy and your tactics are badly flawed. But that's as maybe; that's your affair, and if you press on you'll suffer the consequences. What you haven't told us — '

' — What you haven't told us,' Rafe said forcefully, 'is what the hell we're doing here. What exactly do you want from us, Sangster?'

# 11

They were allocated the nearest cabin. When they'd stripped the rigs from their horses and turned them loose in the corral adjoining the cabin, they walked into a single room sparsely furnished with a couple of wooden cots, cornhusk mattresses, an iron stove, a shaky table and even shakier chairs. Provisions — mostly canned sardines — were on dusty shelves hanging precariously from the walls. A pile of wood crawling with insects was stacked by the stove.

'Seen worse, seen better,' Seth said, tossing his saddle against the wall, 'but it sure ain't home.'

'We'll get there. There's just one small chore to get finished, and I'd say we're about halfway there.'

'Halfway? If we are, that first half was the easy bit.'

Seth was now sitting on the edge of one of the cots, bouncing gently up and down to hear it creak. Rafe had both hands on the table and was leaning forward to stare pensively out of the window. He had a clear view down to the camp-fire. Sangster was still there, still talking.

'That man,' he said, 'doesn't realize what he's up against.'

'The Laramie brothers,' Seth said, deadpan. 'Cross them at your peril.'

'He thinks he's got a hold over us,' Rafe went on, watching Sangster mount his palomino. 'He thinks that we think that they think — '

'Whoa there, turn, spit, then start again.'

Rafe rolled his eyes. 'He thinks that we believe the law still sees us as bank robbers; with his assistance, we eluded a posse that had pursued us to Greybull. All he has to do, he believes, is threaten to hand us over to the law, and we'll meekly do his bidding.'

'Which is using our military experience to plan various robberies across the territory of Wyoming.'

Rafe nodded, stood up straight and folded his arms. Sangster had ridden off towards the hole in the rock face. The outlaws were talking amongst themselves, and Rafe continued to keep an eye on the group by the creek as they began to disperse.

'That's what Sangster wants us to do, yes,' he said. 'That's the bright idea that hit him when he caught sight of us in the livery barn wearing these Confederate jackets.' Rafe plucked at the faded material with finger and thumb. 'It came to him in a flash. He'd got the perfect hideout. He'd got his enlisted men organized: outlaws he knew from way back were riding to join him and form a merry band. And suddenly, in front of him and in deep trouble, were the officers he needed to run the show.'

'But between him riding off into the hills, and us rushing to join him, we were got at,' Seth said. 'Not only was our innocence proved, we were signed

146

up by the opposition; we're working for the other side.'

'Mm. Or working out exactly how we do work for them.'

'Which, as I mentioned, could prove difficult.'

'Well, we'd better think fast, because three of those fellers are walking up the slope.'

Like a cat, Seth rolled off the cot and came up on his feet facing the door. Two steps sideways, and he was part shielded by the iron stove. Rafe stepped around the table so that it would be between him and anyone entering the cabin. That put him with his back to the wall.

The door was hanging off its hinges. A shadow fell across the threshold. A tall man ducked his head as he entered the shack. It was the lanky outlaw festooned with weapons: a knife in a fringed leather sheath dangled against his groin; a six-gun was tied to each thigh; the bone hilt of another knife jutted from one of his stovepipe boots.

He was followed in by a grey-haired man whose face was ravaged by time, another who was stocky and muscular and twenty years younger. Rafe guessed that both would be dangerous after their own fashion; instinctively he knew who they were.

The outlaw draped in armament wore a grin like a knife scar. He wandered across the room, ignored Seth and absently swung a kick at the stove.

'My name's Dane Jagger. I'm running the show here.' He watched Rafe steadily, let that sink in, waited a few moments for the argument that never came. 'Let me introduce you to two fellows who want to shake your hands. The old-timer's Milo Crane. The one looking like an out-of-work cowboy's Lake Rafferty. Come to think of it, I suppose you could say they're both out of work, as of yesterday morning.'

'But not for long,' Rafferty said. He cast a critical eye over Rafe. 'Something was said about shaking hands. You don't appear too keen to shake mine.'

'Maybe I'm particular.'

Rafferty nodded. 'We were in a hurry to put Alamo behind us, but when the pack following us seemed to be slowing we hung back to see what was going on. You led that posse a merry dance, drew them away from us. For that, I thank you. But I'm wondering what you were doing in that part of Wyoming.'

'A bit of this, a bit of that.'

'And you'd arrived there from . . . ?'

'South.'

'South.' Again Rafferty nodded. 'So if you'd ridden up from the south, you'd've been heading . . . ?'

'North.'

'Yeah.' Rafferty grinned. 'You're not only particular, you're vague in your answers.'

'And you're not heading north now,' Dane Jagger said. 'You've been roped in by Mort Sangster. He says you're going to show us how to rob banks.'

'That's the general idea.'

'Ever robbed a bank?'

149

'I've been inside banks,' Rafe said, 'before today.'

'We've all been inside banks,' Jagger said, and he grinned at his two companions. 'Some of us came out rich, some of us came out poor. How about you two fellows?'

'Yeah, we came out,' Seth said, joining the conversation from his position of relaxed nonchalance alongside the stove. 'And here we are.'

'A funny man,' Jagger said.

'But truthful,' Seth said, 'and in no way vague. We came out, and no posse pursued us — you can make of that what you will; draw your own conclusions as to what we were doing in there that made our departure so painless. The point is, we're here to show you how you can do the same.'

Rafe, listening to him, was highly amused. Seth moved away from the shelter of the stove, and again sat on the bed. He was entering into the spirit of the game — if a deadly serious situation could be so called. It would be interesting, Rafe thought, to see where he was leading, and to discover if he, Rafe, could follow his lead without upsetting the applecart.

'You see,' Seth continued, 'my brother there was a respected officer in the Army of the Confederacy — '

'Damn Johnny Reb,' Rafferty said, and turned away to spit.

' — and as such,' Seth went on, unfazed, 'he is able to bring military tactics — '

'The rebels lost the war,' Jagger pointed out.

'Any officer, win or lose,' Rafe said, 'is still twice as efficient as a civilian.'

'Rafferty and Crane have been robbing banks for a while now; they robbed the Alamo bank yesterday, and got clean away,' Jagger said. 'How can you do better? Why should we tamper with a winning streak because Sangster says so and you've got big ideas?'

Seth grinned. 'You just asked and answered your own question.'

'Sangster?' Jagger shook his head.

'We'll listen to Sangster, because he's got inside information so he knows when cash is being moved. But that's all we'll listen to: he'll name the bank; we'll carry out the raid. That's him and us. We don't *need* you.'

'Wrong,' Seth said. 'You need all the help you can get. Look, if the bank's safe is full, security is sure to be tight. The town marshal will be alert and watchful. He'll probably post extra deputies as lookouts. A lock-down situation like that, you ride in cold you're as good as dead. But supposing two experienced military men ride into town ahead of you boys, and assess the situation? We can report back to you, put you in the picture; you decide to go ahead, or say to hell with it and walk away.'

Jagger growled his dissent. 'There's always a way in.'

'Yeah,' Seth said, 'and I can tell you one the military might use. You ever heard of a diversion, or diversionary tactics?'

'Go talk to your grandmother,' Jagger said, sneering. 'I was using those methods when I was still at school.'

'Surprises me you ever went,' Seth said with a faint smile. 'OK, so we — that's me and Rafe — we create a diversion on the other side of town to draw attention away from the bank. Start arguing early in the day, let it develop into open aggression so the town marshal begins to take notice. Then, minutes before you boys ride in, we start fighting: fists, then pistols, and we're so crazy wild there's a clear danger ordinary folk will get hurt.'

Listening, watching the expressions on the outlaws' faces, Rafe found it hard not to laugh out loud.

Rafferty was frowning.

'All that does is get you locked up.'

Seth shook his head. 'No, that's not all. OK, we'll spend a day in a cell, then get tossed into the street. But in the meantime you boys have robbed the bank and are long gone, clear of town without a hitch, basking in the sunshine here in the lost valley.'

Rafferty and Crane exchanged glances. Rafe could see that, somewhat grudgingly, they were coming around to Seth's way of thinking. Jagger was biting his lip. He paced up and down in the confined, crowded space. Expelling breath explosively, he took another kick at the stove and swung around.

'Damn it,' he said, 'we need to talk to Sangster, get this straightened out.'

Crane, the oldest man in the room, was looking placid.

'No need,' he said. 'Rafferty knows my philosophy: if you're going to rob a bank, ride into town looking like a fresh-faced choir boy. We did that in Alamo, and we'll do it again — but knowing for certain every lawman in town's looking the other way will be one hell of a bonus.'

'Maybe,' Jagger said.

He sees it makes sense, but he's the man running this, the big chief, and he's reluctant to admit Seth's right, Rafe thought. He stepped aside, saw

Jagger kick the loose-hanging door on his way out, and turned to the window to watch all three men walk down the slope towards the creek.

'I've never in my life,' he said without turning, 'heard such a load of bullshit.'

Seth chuckled. 'I've been following the wrong calling. I should have been an outlaw.'

'Or a writer of lurid fiction. But you're not the only man dreaming impossible dreams.'

He turned, again leaned back against the table.

'Know who I'm talking about?'

Sure,' Seth nodded. 'Mort 'King' Sangster.'

'Damn right,' Rafe said. 'That man may know the best banks to hit and when to do it, but if he thinks he's got these outlaws in his pocket then I'm the next president of the United States.'

# 12

That morning, after his talk with the Laramie brothers, Kieran Stark rode out of Greybull. But instead of heading south towards Alamo — his stated intention, but a tale told deliberately to deceive his listeners — Stark headed north and a little west towards the Shoshone River. The river formed the natural northern boundary of the Circle C ranch owned by Joseph Corrigan. Kieran Stark wasn't quite sure about the location of the other boundaries, but he did know that the Circle C covered a vast area — and Corrigan was an old man.

Joseph Corrigan was unmarried. He had no heirs. His wealth lay in property, and the vast herds roaming his pastures.

Kieran Stark was hypnotized by the possibilities. But, more than that, he knew he was rapidly running out of time.

The yard was almost deserted when he rode in. The foreman was emerging from the bunkhouse. He recognized Stark, invited him to step down, and a couple of minutes later Stark was in Corrigan's big living room sipping expensive whiskey from a crystal glass.

Corrigan, in his eighties, had a bald scalp, a face like dried leather but the mind of a highly intelligent thirty year old. He was sitting in a shabby armchair that looked too big for him. From its depths, his watery grey eyes peered knowingly at Stark.

'Nice of you to call. But we both know the real reason you're here. The answer, to avoid wasting time in polite sparring, is unchanged.'

'I'm disappointed.'

'That continues to surprise me. A man with no money cannot buy property the size of Circle C, Mr Stark.'

'The money will be there when you name your price. Cash on the barrel.'

Corrigan raised his eyebrows.

'Now I'm shocked. I know you're always short of money. That leads me to suspect unethical shenanigans. Are you planning on acquiring the necessary cash by illegal methods?'

Stark's grip tightened on the whiskey glass. Frowning, he shook his head.

'How I get the money is none of your business. All you need to know is I will be in a position to buy whenever you decide you're ready to sell — and I'd point out that, at your age, time is running out.'

Corrigan chuckled.

'Are you resorting to the health card, the 'death's dark prevail' card? Are you attempting to sow the seeds of fear in my mind?'

'California has a wonderful climate. The warm sun is kind to old bones, old joints. Let me buy Circle C and you'll have more than enough money to spend your remaining years in luxury on the edge of the Pacific Ocean. Sell, then pamper yourself,

Corrigan. Doesn't that idea tempt you?'

'I have been tempted many times, but never by a conniving trickster like you. And don't talk to me about running out of time; we both know why you're desperate to buy.'

'Circle C is an attractive proposition to any ambitious — '

'You lied your way into the Wyoming Cattlemen's Association top position,' Corrigan went on remorselessly. 'You faked a top university degree; told them you owned a flourishing ranch. Those untruths were quickly uncovered: you're uneducated, and you live in an old and run-down cabin for which you pay rent. As a result of that deliberate deceit, you have until December this year. Then you will be kicked out of your position, and an honest rancher will take your place.'

'If I owned Circle C — '

'No, Mr Stark. You could own the entire territory of Wyoming, and that would not be enough. There is no place

159

for cheats in the association. Come December, you're out on your ear.'

His pulse hammering, Stark tossed back the remains of the whiskey. When he climbed to his feet, he realized his legs were trembling. Fighting his fury, struggling to put a look of unconcern on his face, he turned on the old rancher.

'I respect your decision, of course. But if something should happen — something so serious that you can see selling Circle C as the only way out of a calamitous situation — why, then I'm sure you'll know where to find me. If you don't, you can be sure I will find you.'

With that parting shot, Kieran Stark stormed out.

# 13

The rain was beating down, drumming on the cabin's rotting shingle roof. Drips spattered the dirt floor, and hissed like snakes on the glowing top of the iron stove. Outside, the lost valley was in darkness broken only by the faint light from the other cabins and the occasional brilliant flash of lightning, which revealed the canyon's looming walls and the tumbling white waters of the creek rushing towards the fissure in the cliff face.

'Sangster thinks he's got it all worked out,' Rafe said. 'He hasn't. I've never in my whole life met a more foolish man.'

He was lying on the cot. Seth had abandoned it in favour of a chair by the table. An oil lamp glowed in front of him. He was idly scratching designs on the table top with the point of his knife.

'Yeah. He's a real donkey. He truly

believes outlaws who get their hands on a pile of cash are going to hand the lot over to him.'

'On the other hand,' Rafe said, 'that's exactly what Rafferty and Crane did.'

'The card shark,' Seth said, 'always lets the sucker win the first few hands. They handed it over willingly because they know there's a lot more to come and they want to get their hands on that big pot.'

'Mm. My thoughts exactly.' Fingers laced behind his head, Rafe squinted across at his brother. 'But knowing that Sangster's a fool doesn't help us any.'

'No, but to me it suggests something that's pretty obvious: in all this talk of bank robberies on a grand scale, Sangster cannot be the big chief.'

Startled, Rafe swung his legs off the cot and sat up.

'Really? I don't think that's necessarily true. He could be convinced his schemes are foolproof. The West's got dozens of stories about brainless outlaws who've concocted hair-brained schemes and shot themselves in the foot.'

'I know. But, if you think about it, this scheme's been cleverly worked out. The outlaws have been given a plausible story involving a secret hide-out. Go on from there and I believe it could work in every respect, but fall at the final hurdle when Jagger and his boys are supposed to hand over the money.'

'So that's saying it's not that clever after all.'

'It's clever if you ignore that bit about handing over the money. But that may be a load of bull. Instead, there could be a double-cross: someone's going to take that money off them; they do the dirty work, he snatches the cash and they end up with nothing.'

'You really think Sangster could do that?'

'No, I don't. And that's exactly what I'm saying: there's someone else involved.'

Rafe had his six-gun out. He twirled

it idly on his forefinger, grimaced thoughtfully.

'If you're right, it will work just the once: there can only be the one bank raid, and to make it worthwhile it'd have to be a big one.' He tossed the six-gun onto the thin blankets and stood up. 'You've put some thought into this. What brought it on?'

'The scheme's got a neat twist. Remember what Sangster told us? He knows a man who can tell him when cattle are being moved, when a big herd's being sold, which bank the rancher uses, and the date cash is going in.'

'And?'

'Soon's he said that, I thought of a conversation we had earlier, in town, in the Greybull Palace.'

'Glory be,' Rafe said after a moment's thought. 'You're talking about Kieran Stark. Respected member of the Wyoming Cattlemen's Association.'

'Right, and you know what George

Adams thinks of him.'

For a few minutes there was no more talk. The rain was a constant drumming in the background as Rafe prepared and poured coffee. Thunder rumbled. Sheet lightning lit up the room. Both men drank in silence.

It was Rafe who reopened the discussion.

'Whether there's one man, two, or a whole bunch of them with brains, the next robbery's being planned now. Tomorrow, Sangster — the only man we can be sure we're dealing with — will tell us what he wants us to do. The question is, what do we do? George Adams and John Senior will be chewing their fingernails to the quick. I'd like to let them know what's going on — particularly your suspicions about Stark — but how do we do that?'

'In this weather,' Seth said, 'I reckon we could ride out of here without being seen.'

'Greybull and back before dawn? I think not.'

'Why come back?'

'Damn it, you're right,' Rafe said. 'We've identified the Alamo bank robbers, surely got enough to incriminate Sangster.'

'But not enough to stop the next bank robbery. There's a lot of banks out there. Which one will they hit?'

Rafe grinned. 'That's easy. To commit any robbery, they've got to leave this canyon. There's only one way out. When they take it, they'll be tracked every inch of the way.'

★ ★ ★

They left the battered oil lamp burning on the table, turning up the wick and moving the light closer to the window. Then, donning their slickers, they heaved their rigs onto their shoulders and stepped out into the wet, dark night.

'With the corral so close, the first bit's easy,' Rafe said, standing back against the cabin as the wind buffeted.

'After that it's a ride across open space, all the way to the creek and the hole in the wall.'

'Seems to me we're making a habit of fording rivers,' Seth said. 'Mostly when they're in spate.'

'Well, as I can't rightly recall when you last had a wash,' Rafe said, 'doing it one more time doesn't seem like a bad idea.'

It took them but a few minutes to call softly to their horses, saddle up and climb aboard. Lights still gleamed in cabin windows, but there was no sign of any movement. Once, Rafe thought he heard harsh laughter, but the sound was swallowed up in a rumble of thunder. The flash of lightning that followed revealed the daunting ride that lay ahead of them. The grassy slopes were slick. The creek was a tumbling flood of white water. At its eastern end, the water boiled up against the cliff face as, each second, thousands of gallons of run-off were forced into the fissure.

'We could drown,' Seth said.

'I'm already drowning just sitting here,' Rafe said. 'Come on, let's get it done.'

With a flick of the reins he started his horse down the slope. The animal was pleased to be moving. Though made nervous by the thunder and lightning, it nevertheless picked its way delicately across the slippery ground. Expecting at any moment the roars of anger that would mean their departure had been noticed, the Laramie brothers moved cautiously but steadily away from the cabins.

'We crossed that creek to get here,' Seth said, drawing level, 'but it strikes me there's no need to do that: like it or not, we're going into that hole no matter which side of the water we're on.'

Down the slope they went. They reached the creek's south bank. With the wind whipping, flying spray chill on the back of their necks, they made it halfway to the fissure. Then came the sound they'd been dreading: a faint crack that was all too familiar and had nothing to do with the stormy weather. It was followed by a second, a third — and then a furious volley of shots rang out.

Something buzzed uncomfortably close to Rafe's ear. He cast a hasty glance backwards. A cabin door was open. By the light leaking over the threshold he saw a man standing with a rifle, another a little way to his left. Both weapon fired again, the muzzle flashes winking red in the darkness. The bullets, Rafe judged, flew well wide.

'I'll lay odds that's Jagger,' he called to Seth. 'Him with the arsenal. He's got another man with him. Pity they spotted us, but I think they're way too late.'

His words were lost in the wild night. Seth had blazed on by, his shiny slicker flapping like a giant bat's wings. Without hesitation he sent his horse plunging into the maelstrom that was the entrance to the fissure. Water boiled around the blue roan's flanks. Rafe saw its head toss, saw Seth's hand raised high, thought he heard a yell followed by a shrill whinny. Then he, too, was charging into the fissure and suddenly he was up to his waist in icy water and beneath him, a mass of fighting muscle, his horse was struggling to turn back.

But the immense pressure behind them was too great. The blackness inside the fissure was the blackness of death. Foaming water rose to Rafe's face and began choking him. He felt the horse's hoofs leave the ground. By the twisting of its body between his legs he knew it was kicking desperately. It was trying to swim, but swimming was impossible. As the helpless horse was carried bodily by the water, Rafe slammed into the rock face. His shoulder was ripped by a bolt of agony. He groaned through clenched teeth. The groan expelled precious air. Gasping, wheezing, struggling to draw breath, he inhaled icy water. Immediately he vomited. Weakness washed through his body. His knees began to lose their grip on the wet saddle. Frantically, he gripped the horn and hung on.

How long did that nightmare ride last? To Rafe it felt like eternity. In fact, it could have been no more than thirty seconds from the time they entered the fissure to their violent ejection at the western opening. The flood waters shot from the confines of the fissure, dissipated, weakened. Rafe's startled horse found itself once more standing, quivering but alive. It shook itself like a dog, moved forward through deep, fast-flowing water that had lost all its terrors. Within seconds it was on muddy ground, and Rafe was guiding it along the twisting path through the trees. When he emerged, behind Sangster's cabin, Seth was waiting.

'I don't want to worry you,' he said, 'but I think I took a slug.'

Even as he spoke he slumped wearily forward in the saddle to lie, limp and clinging, along the blue roan's neck.

171

* * *

The rain had turned the flow of blood from Seth's wound pink and watery. In the meagre shelter of the trees on the far side of the clearing — with the distant, shimmering light from Sangster's cabin window an ever-present warning that they were not yet clear — Rafe helped his brother down from the roan and sat him comfortably against a massive log. When he removed the slicker and ripped away the shirt to reveal the wound, he took a deep, shuddering breath of relief.

'The bullet broke the skin, sliced across muscle, caused no lasting harm,' he said. 'A lot of blood, but in the army they'd call your over-reaction malingering and throw you in the hoosegow.'

He rose to fetch a clean bandanna from his saddlebag, quickly returned and dressed and strapped the bloody wound. Seth appeared to be grinning, but it was a fixed grimace of pain. On his forehead the sheen of sweat was visible despite the rainwater trickling down from hair plastered to his scalp. He gasped when Rafe straightened his clothing and replaced the wet slicker. For a moment his head fell forward limply. When he lifted it, the grimace had been replaced by a look of fiery determination.

'You've been playing the medic, I've been doing my bit by keeping an eye on that cabin — '

'Like hell you have — '

' — and, would you believe it, those fellows doing all that shooting were crazy enough to follow us through that hole in the wall? Sangster's door's open. All three of them are on the gallery, looking this way.'

Quickly, Rafe squinted across the rain-swept clearing, and suddenly he was grinning.

'Hadn't we already decided he was a fool? Hell, this confirms it, him and those crazy outlaws, because nobody army trained would bunch up and expose themselves like that.'

Even as he was talking Rafe had moved to his tethered horse and slipped his Winchester from the saddle boot. He walked to the fringe of the woods, leaned his battered left shoulder against a tree to steady himself, then jacked a shell into the breech and fired three aimed shots at the distant cabin.

The reaction was laughable.

The cold steel of rifle barrels glinted in the lamplight as two of the men spun one way, then the other, then dropped flat on the boards. The third — undoubtedly Morton Sangster — turned, ran into the cabin and slammed the door.

'Job done,' Rafe said. 'Come on, let's get you onto that horse. They'll be up again very soon, shamefaced and ready to give chase. By the time they do that, I want to be halfway to Greybull.'

# 14

They rode into town at a canter, passing the silent Greybull Palace without a sideways glance and continuing down the slope to pull in at the hitch rail outside George Adams's jail. They both dismounted stiffly, nursing shoulders damaged in different ways but equally painful.

When they tramped water and mud into the lamplit office, Adams was dozing in his chair, his stockinged feet up on the desk.

'Glory be,' he said, blinking owlishly. 'A couple of drowned rats. Which sinking ship have you deserted?'

'Where's John Senior?' Rafe said.

'In the only rooming-house we've got, and snoring his head off if he's got any sense.'

'I'll go roust him out of there,' Seth said, weariness and shock thickening his voice.

The door slammed behind him.

'Sounds urgent,' Adams said, yawning.

'The bit you'll be interested in possibly confirms what you already suspect. We need Senior here because the men we've left up there in the canyon are going to move fast.' Rafe slipped awkwardly out of his slicker, hung it over a chair. 'You said something about Kieran Stark lying through his teeth to secure his current position; what else do you know about him?'

'Nothing. He came on the scene some eighteen months ago. Talk is he got close to Mort Sangster, but I've never seen them together.'

'OK. So, keep your mind fixed on what you *know* he does, and listen to this. Mort Sangster appears to be planning a series of bank raids. There's a safe hideout for the robbers: at the top of that box canyon he lives in, there's a way through the cliffs into a hidden valley. Sangster has been able to

176

recruit a number of outlaws for his scheme — '

The door crashed open. John Senior walked in, nodded to Rafe and stepped aside for a bone-weary Seth to enter and slump into a chair.

'Adams will fill you in later,' Rafe said to Senior. 'What I was about to say,' he went on, turning again to Adams, 'is that Sangster was able to pull in those men because he knows when herds are being sold, who's doing the selling, and the banks where the money will end up.'

There was a heavy silence. Adams was frowning and shaking his head.

'Sangster knows?'

'Let's say he *gets* to know,' Rafe said — and waited.

'The only way he could do that,' John Senior said, 'is by talking to the ranchers themselves, or by talking to someone working for — '

'The Cattlemen's Association,' George Adams said, and sat bolt upright in his chair. 'Kieran Stark.'

'We reached the conclusion,' Seth said, 'that Mort Sangster's a fool. That's led us to believe that there has to be someone pulling his strings. Stark's the obvious first choice. I also said Sangster appears to be planning a series of raids. What's more likely is one big raid, then a double-cross leaving the outlaws who pull it empty-handed.'

Adams nodded. 'And Stark and Sangster — if you're right — very rich indeed.'

Rafe nodded. He looked at Senior. 'When we were all in the café, you said you were heading for Alamo. In the saloon, Stark told us he was going to Alamo in his official capacity; he wanted to talk to that man who got a clear view of the bank robbers. Do you know if he did that?'

Senior's face was grim. 'That's exactly what he didn't do. We left Greybull at about the same time. I headed for Alamo, and I know damn well Stark went the other way: he rode north.'

'For a talk with his front man, Mort Sangster,' Seth suggested. 'And the men who pulled the Alamo raid.' He looked at Senior. 'We identified them for sure. There's six men there. Two called Crane and Rafferty did the Alamo job.'

Senior looked elated. George Adams was up on his feet.

'You said those outlaws will move fast. What does that mean.'

'They saw us break out of the valley, followed, damn near killed Seth,' Rafe said. 'They know Sangster spilled everything to us; they'll know we were heading into town to pass that information on to you.'

'So they'll want to hit a bank before George can act,' Senior said.

Adams nodded. 'But they could hit just about any bank in the territory: Basin, Lovell, Cowley — even here in Greybull. How do we find out which one? If we talk to Stark, he'll deny everything, and it's surely too late to tackle Sangster.'

'Well, those outlaws have got to come

out of their hideout if they want to rob any bank,' Rafe said, 'and as there's only the one way out of that canyon — '

'We ride up there, wait, then follow them,' Adams said, catching on at once and grinning happily.

'We'll need to be out early,' Senior said. 'If we're right, Stark will point to a bank loaded with cash. It could be a long ride.'

'Yeah, and that means we all need sleep,' Rafe said.

Senior frowned. 'You really don't need to be in this,' he said. 'We were already pretty sure you had nothing to do with that Alamo raid. Locating the real bank robbers in that hidden valley puts the seal on your innocence. Surely you should be heading home?'

'You've only got our word those bank robbers are out there; I'd like to be there when you make the arrest.' Rafe grinned. 'Besides, Lovell and Cowley take us a goodly way in the right direction.'

'Well, you're right about one thing,

we need sleep,' Adams said. 'Trouble is, we're not going to get much. Even though we know Kieran Stark is going to protest his innocence, I do want to talk to him before we head out, see what he has to say for himself. To cram everything in, we'll need to leave here well before first light.'

Seth struggled out of the chair, groaning.

'The mere thought of it gives me a headache. Whoever's doing early calls will find me in my favourite cell. Don't worry, I won't be too disappointed if I don't wake up and you leave without me.'

# 15

The next morning Rafe and Seth stayed in town while George Adams and John Senior rode out in the grey pre-dawn. A five-minute ride through the grey half-light brought them to the cabin on the outskirts of Greybull. Stark answered their knock and invited them into the run-down dwelling that, inside, was surprisingly neat and tidy.

George Adams tackled the Cattlemen's Association official, detailing all of the Laramie brothers' suspicions.

Stark, clearing away his breakfast dishes while listening, was highly amused.

'I can understand your concern,' he said, 'but let me assure you, they're wrong. If Mort Sangster's getting that kind of information, it does not come from me. And if he's recruiting outlaws for a series of bank robberies, that's certainly news I'll pass on to those likely to be concerned.'

'But you do know Sangster?'

Stark curled his lip. 'Doesn't everybody know the man who calls himself King?'

'Yeah, but what about your reputation?' John Senior said, moving away from the door and further into the room. 'From what I've heard, you got your present position by unfair means.'

Stark, housekeeping all finished, was shrugging into his jacket. He paused and frowned at Senior's accusation.

'If you mean by deceit, my answer to that is, look at my record in the association. Never mind how I got there, or the kind of man I might have been in the past: study my performance over the past nine months. Also, bear in mind that I have several influential ranchers who trust me implicitly. Joe Corrigan's one. I spoke to him yesterday, at his spread on the Shoshone. The man is old, and he's tired. He's getting out, he wants to sell Circle

C, and he's looking favourably at an offer I made.'

'You?' George Adams was looking about him in exaggerated astonishment. 'Where in hell are you getting that kind of money?'

'A black sheep,' Stark said, 'often has rich relatives, resources accumulated during a life walking a thin line, or grand designs beyond the understanding of ordinary folk.'

With that veiled insult delivered he straightened his jacket, fixed his string tie and looked challengingly at the two lawmen. As he did so there was a look on his face that had a worm of unease stirring uncomfortably inside John Senior.

Was their thinking muddled? Were they being led by the nose by a man out-thinking them every step of the way?

As he followed Adams out to their horses and deliberately stood fiddling with his rig while Stark mounted up and — surprise, surprise — set off in a northerly direction, the glances he and the Greybull marshal exchanged were singularly lacking in confidence.

★ ★ ★

*Two hours later.*

'I've been foolish,' Morton Sangster said. 'A sudden rush of blood to the head and, you were right, I saw in the Laramie brothers a reflection of you and me as things might have been. So I invited them into the set-up, ended up revealing just about everything we've discussed. They absorbed the lot, added their own interpretation, and took it all to town.' He took a deep breath. 'My foolishness — and it's jeopardized your grand scheme.'

'Not a chance.'

Kieran Stark had ridden up the canyon at a good pace, but without undue haste. His horse was tied at the hitch rail. Standing on the gallery, looking down across the misty clearing, Stark was supremely relaxed. He had a cigar in his hand. His black jacket was swept back, exposing his white shirt and string tie. He was, Sangster thought, almost beaming — and Sangster couldn't understand why.

'Not only that,' Sangster said huskily, 'but you were right about the . . . about the other. On that terrible night, so long ago, there was no band of renegades. That was a story I made up for your benefit. Reality is, the killing was done by me.'

He felt immense relief when the confession was out, but still looked with trepidation at his brother.

Stark shrugged. 'I've always known,' he said. 'I was awake that night. Six years old, but I heard the ructions. I got out of bed and saw everything.'

'Sweet Jesus,' Sangster moaned, appalled.

'And I've always known why you acted the way you did. Ma and Pa, they used to tell me what was going on. 'Leave it', they'd say, if I grabbed a broom, or picked up the water pail, 'your useless brother, he does the work around here'.' Stark grinned. 'So you can bet your life I played on that. Why bother with chores, when there's a live-in slave?'

'Nevertheless, my act put you in orphanages, in numerous foster homes where you were treated cruelly.'

'Relax,' Stark said. 'Let me tell you, in my adult life I've done much worse than anything you can imagine. You and me, in our separate ways, we've roamed the West fleecing suckers, taking from the meek, always two steps ahead of the law. Orphans, we came up the hard way, learned the hard way. And now I look at it this way: everything I've done, everything you've done, has been leading up to what we are about to do together in the next couple of days.'

'Us? Together?'

'Sure, you and me. Together. Why else would I have tracked you down?'

'And the others? The men I've brought in with promises? The men who'll pull off the bank raid dreaming of pockets stuffed with greenbacks?'

'Forget them,' Stark said bluntly. 'Pull up a chair, sit down with me, then forget everything you've heard from me — '

'The other day — '

'That's in the past, gone, forgotten. When we spoke I was treating you like a cur, but, more importantly, I was feeding you false information. I wanted you to believe without question what those outlaws believed, because that way there could be no slip up: it would be impossible for you to give the game away, because you didn't know the nature of the game. All right, that's done. This time, what I say is for your ears only. So, sit back and listen in amazement while I tell you what's really going on here.'

# 16

The heavy rain had died away over-night. The sun's first brilliant rays were slanting over the peaks of the Bighorn Mountains, their warmth already lifting mist from the wet grass and the swollen creeks and rivers. Deep in a stand of dark trees with the thick canopy of leaves blocking much of the light, the air was damp and chill. Waiting impatiently, still astride their horses lest they be caught unawares, the two lawmen and the Laramie brothers were shivering, now and then rubbing their hands or swinging their arms to keep warm.

They had been there an hour when Rafe Laramie was jerked from an uncomfortable half-doze. He stirred, and cocked his head.

'I think I hear them,' he said.

Seth, too, had caught the drum of

hoofs. The four men eased their mounts forward and watched from their place of concealment as six outlaws emerged from Sangster's box canyon and, harness jingling, rode off in a direction slightly to the north of west.

'That rules out raids on the banks in Manderson, Basin or Greybull,' George Adams said.

'We bow to your wisdom and local knowledge,' John Senior said. 'So what does that mean, either Lovell or Cowley?'

'Yeah, one or the other. They're split by the Shoshone River, Lovell to the south, Cowley some twenty miles to the north on the edge of the Bighorn lake. Both have privately owned banks. Both are surrounded by rich cattle country. There's a few prosperous ranches out there.'

'OK, so we give them time to get clear, then get on their tails,' Senior said. 'Now we've got a fair idea where they're heading, if we lose them it won't be a disaster.'

Adams snorted. 'That won't happen. There must be a good slice of Indian in me, 'cos nobody I've trailed has ever given me the slip.'

By mid-morning as, from a rise, they watched the outlaws swim their horses across the Bighorn River, he was announcing with confidence that they were going to hit the bank in Lovell.

'You reading their minds from a distance?' Senior said.

'Naw. Lovell's been my favourite from the outset. It's got a bigger bank. Most of the important ranchers use it.'

'Then I think you're right. Stark brought up Joe Corrigan's name when he was talking to us. We should have picked that up. He must know for sure Corrigan's recently banked a heap of money, and the name slipped out because it was burning a hole in his brain.'

Adams hesitated. 'I'm not sure about Corrigan. Does he bank there?'

He was putting the question to himself, obviously couldn't come up with the answer, and shrugged.

'Doesn't matter,' he said. 'Other ranchers surely do, and that's enough for me — and for Stark, I'd say.'

Rafe, who had kept quiet for most of the ride, now chipped in.

'Talking of Stark, where is he? Him *and* Sangster? Back at the canyon, waiting for the merry band to return? Or what?'

'Yeah, that's been bothering me,' John Senior said. 'What the hell is he up to?'

'The easy answer is, yes, he's back in the lost valley these fellers discovered,' Adams said. 'If he really is the man with the information, the man directing operations, then that's where he's sure to be.'

'Waiting for the return of the bank robbers,' Senior said, nodding. 'What's the hard answer, George?'

'That we're wrong,' Rafe Laramie said. 'George thinks there's a faint chance Kieran Stark's everything he says he is, and we're accusing an innocent man.'

'We know he lies,' Senior said. 'He said he was riding to Alamo — '

'Means nothing,' Rafe said. 'A man can change his mind.'

'Yeah, but all of this,' Seth Laramie said scathingly, 'has got absolutely nothing to do with what's going on here in front of us. According to George, those six men putting distance between them and us are going to carry out an armed raid on the Lovell bank, and empty the safe. So what the hell are we doing sitting here talking about Kieran Stark?'

And with that he touched the blue roan with his spurs and rode like the wind down the long slope to the Bighorn River.

★   ★   ★

'Every damn one of those outlaws knows you two by sight,' John Senior said. 'That's going to make it difficult when we ride in.'

'They'll be concentrating on the bank

and their immediate surroundings,' Rafe Laramie said, 'not studying faces. Besides, there's more than one way into town. What we do is split up and go in from four different directions. But we make it fast, because those fellers are going in now, and they'll be all fired up.'

They had pushed on hard after Seth, splashing across the river and cautiously closing in on the outlaws as they neared the town of Lovell. There had been some discussion as they rode about what they were going to do.

George Adams had been all for charging in ahead of the outlaws, alerting the bank and forming a protective shield. John Senior had smiled. He'd pointed out that doing it that way would keep the bank's money in the safe, but it wouldn't break up the gang: the outlaws would simply ride on by, innocent bystanders, and live to fight another day; Sangster and Stark — if he was involved — would revise their plans.

Now he nodded, clearly liking Rafe's idea.

'Let's do it,' he said, his eyes alight. 'We'll go in from the four points of the compass, homing in on the bank.'

'Which is easy done,' George Adams said, 'because the bank's in the square, and the square's in the middle of town.'

'Final point,' Rafe said, 'and I leave this decision to you officers of the law. Are we stopping them before they go in, or when they come out?'

Adams took a deep breath.

'Waiting until they come out is risking lives inside the bank. Stopping them before they go in raises the same objection: they'll have done nothing, committed no crime, we'll have nothing on them.'

'There's your answer, Rafe,' Senior said.

'We work this right, we'll have formed a half-circle of armed men well away from the front of the bank,' Adams said. 'We watch, and we wait. When they come bursting out we have rifles at the ready, and we step out of our hiding places and challenge them. I don't expect them to roll over: there's going to be shooting, and men are going to go down.' He paused, looked at each of the other men in turn. 'Any questions?'

There was none.

'Right, so with that the talking's all done,' Adams said. 'Let's go get them.'

★   ★   ★

Despite the prolonged discussion, all four of them reached the square before the bank robbers. Rafe Laramie put that down to the six men slowing and becoming more cautious, probably extremely jittery, as they entered Lovell and the minutes and seconds ticked away. As they approached the square, and the bank, their eyes would be everywhere. They would not be studying faces, but they would see a badge glittering on every man's vest, suspicion in every man's eyes, the threat of sudden death every time a man's hand absently brushed his six-gun.

Their nerves would be as tight as violin strings singing a warning. They would be very, very dangerous.

Rafe rode in from the east, cutting down a narrow alley between business premises. From the end of the alley he could see across the sun-baked square. The bank was an imposing stone building sandwiched between a general store and a gunsmith's shop. A flight of worn stone steps led up to the heavy door. In the centre of the square there was a water trough, and Rafe guessed the town's livery barn would be nearby. The jail, he knew from George Adams, was on the other side of town. In the wrong place for the Lovell town marshal: resourceful and quick-witted outlaws could be in and out of the bank and leaving town before he came running to the sound of gunfire.

Shops and businesses were open, but there were not many people about. After the heavy rains, the day was unusually hot. The square was a sea of drying mud from which rose a foul-smelling miasma. Even though horsemen and lumbering wagons were passing through, an air of lethargy hung over the town.

Though he couldn't see him, Rafe knew Seth was in an identical alley across the square. It opened on the far side of the gunsmith's shop, putting that premises between the alley and the bank. George Adams was also somewhere on the square's perimeter, staying under cover.

John Senior, taking advantage of the town's layout, rode boldly into the square, dismounted, and began watering his horse at the trough.

His eyes were everywhere. He was standing close to his horse. His Winchester was in its boot, but close to his hand.

Even as Senior's horse dipped its head, the six outlaws appeared on the far side of the square. Using their heads, they had drifted apart so that it was not obvious they were a united group. Rafferty and Crane were out in front, well separated from the others. They, led by Jagger, were hanging back and looking about them in so casual a manner that it was almost laughable.

Feeling a sudden quickening of his pulse Rafe eased out of the saddle, threw the reins over his horse's head so they trailed and stopped the animal from walking away. Then he slipped his rifle out of its boot and stepped to the corner of the building at the end of the alley.

And now he could see Seth. Across the square, their eyes met. Rafe nodded, then returned his gaze to the outlaws.

Six men. Too many, too obvious; they were going about it the wrong way. Then, watching, it became clear to Rafe that just two men would be involved in the robbery: Rafferty and Crane, riding their luck. They rode unhurriedly towards the bank. Both men dismounted. Crane held the horses.

Rafferty hitched his belt, then climbed the steps to the bank and disappeared in the gloom of its interior.

Jagger rode with another man to the side of the square opposite the bank. That put them close to Rafe's position. The other two outlaws, whose names Rafe did not know, rode across to the horse trough. Without dismounting, they allowed their horses to step daintily forward and dip their muzzles into the cool water.

Those two men began talking to John Senior.

Across the square, Seth stepped up onto the blue roan, and rode out to join the three men at the water trough.

'Glory be,' Rafe breathed.

As he waited for what he considered inevitable — the sound of shots from the bank — he was aware of being acutely alert. Within him there was mounting tension. The various factions had moved into positions that gave clear advantage to the lawmen and to him and Seth. Everything was running smoothly — too damn smoothly. Yet sensing that there must, surely, be something wrong, still Rafe couldn't believe their luck. With the advantage of surprise, Senior and Seth could easily handle the two at the trough. Rafe was confident he could take Jagger and the other man, who were now mere yards away from his position and unaware that they were in danger. That left Crane, and Rafferty when he came charging out with the money, to George Adams — and in his present mood, big George could probably take them with his bare hands.

Rafe was still smiling at the picture that conjured up when the bank's door banged open and Rafferty came tumbling down the steps. He had a six-gun in his hand. It glittered in the hot sun. His other hand was empty. Even from across the square Rafe could see that the man was furious. His eyes were staring, his face was glistening and red. As he leaped from the bottom step he yelled something to Crane. Then he ran for his horse as Crane dropped the reins he'd been holding and began to swing his own mount away from the bank.

George Adams sprang into action.

Wherever the Greybull marshal had been waiting, he had stayed mounted. Suddenly he was there, out in the sunlight and charging across the caked and muddy square. He was using his knees to control his big chestnut gelding. Half turned in the saddle, he held a Winchester rifle in both hands. It was pointing in the general direction of Rafferty and Crane.

'Stand still!' he roared. 'You're both under arrest for attempted bank robbery.'

'Damn it,' Rafe whispered.

As he stepped swiftly out of the alley, he witnessed an explosion of violent action at the water trough. When George Adams's bellow sent ragged crows flapping from the roof of the bank, the two outlaws hesitated for but a fraction of a second. Then they wrenched on the reins to lift their horses' heads away from the water, raked flesh cruelly with spurs and tried to spin their mounts on a dime.

Like lightning, Seth drew his six-gun and sent his big blue roan leaping to block their path. Behind them, Senior drew his rifle and leaped forward. A high, wide swing with the Winchester slammed the barrel against the side of a naked neck. Something snapped, and the outlaw toppled from the saddle like a falling log.

Seth loudly cocked his six-gun. Holding it with both hands high, he was grinning as he deliberately took aim at the bridge of the outlaw's nose. Eyes wild, the man glanced swiftly left and right. His horse was dancing skittishly, its head straining upwards, neck stretched and eyes rolling as it tried to back away from Seth's roan. But there was now a riderless horse blocking it from behind. The outlaw was reaching for his six-gun but struggling to hold the horse and stay in the saddle; his companion was down on the ground, motionless, leaking blood. With a scowl, the man realized the game was up. He let his shoulder muscles relax. Then he spat his disgust, and lifted his hands shoulder high.

Jagger and the other man weren't hanging about.

As Rafe stepped out of the alley and turned to where he knew they'd been waiting, he was in time to see them spurring their horses away from the action. Jagger was hunched forward in the saddle, going like the wind along the edge of the plank walk with his various weapons flapping. His companion was moving much slower, but doing so deliberately: Rafe knew he had his eyes on the entrance to an alley just ahead of him, and was about to slip away.

Rafe braced his legs, drove the butt of his rifle into his shoulder. Ignoring for a moment the racing Jagger, he managed one shot at the nearer outlaw. A black Stetson went flying. Then the man swung his horse into the alley, and was gone.

Jagger was rapidly approaching the far end of the square. Rafe dropped to one knee. Bracing his elbows, he fired another, well-aimed shot. It hit home. The outlaw arched backwards in the saddle. Then he fell. He hit the ground with both shoulders. One foot caught in a stirrup. Limp, flopping, all life gone from his body, he was dragged out of the square by the terrified horse.

George Adams was in trouble.

As he approached the bank, Rafferty and Crane turned to face him. A rifle is excellent for long range work, but when a man is mounted on a racing horse that weapon becomes almost useless. Adams was an experienced lawman. He knew very quickly he had made a mistake. The Winchester glittered as he threw it from him and it spun end over end into the mud. As soon as it left his hand, he was reaching for his six-gun.

He was too late.

A volley of shots rang out as Rafferty

and Crane began firing. Even as he ran for his horse, mounted and started across the square, Rafe heard the fleshy thud as at least one of the bullets hit home, saw the big lawman rear in the saddle and begin to fall.

But now the whole square was alive. From all corners, men drawing their weapons were running towards the bank. Seth had left the outlaw still standing at the water trough to the dismounted John Senior, and was driving his roan hard across the muddy expanse of open ground.

From different directions, Rafe and Seth reached the bank in seconds. George Adams had valiantly grabbed the horn, and the big man was slumped forward but still in the saddle. Rafferty and Crane had fired their volley and were now thinking of their own hides. Looking frantically about them, panicking as they saw the armed men converging on the scene, they were already spurring away when the Laramie brothers caught up.

Rafe got there first. He veered, drove his horse alongside Crane's racing mount. The horses came together with a solid impact. Both men were jolted, then rode thigh to thigh as Rafe leaned his horse hard against the outlaw's ragged pony. Then Rafe swung his six-gun. He managed to deliver but a glancing blow to the man's head. The Stetson afforded some protection, but the blow was heavy enough to leave Crane dazed. The outlaw swayed in the saddle. Gritting his teeth, Rafe leaned across and threw his arms about the man's shoulders. Together they fell between the racing horses. Razor-sharp hoofs flashed inches from Rafe's head. Then the horses had thundered away across the square.

Holding the half-conscious Crane in a headlock, Rafe looked for Rafferty. He was riding hard. Once out of the square, he could run or hide; he would be difficult to apprehend. Rafe opened his mouth to yell to Seth. Then across the square close to where the outlaw was riding, a shot rang out. Without any slackening of speed, Rafferty flung his hands wide and tumbled from his horse. The horse careered onwards, mane and stirrups flying, to disappear into the town's main street.

On the plank walk, a cheer erupted: it had been a citizen of Lovell who had brought down the last outlaw.

John Senior ran up, puffing, as Rafe climbed to his feet. He dragged Crane with him, kept a firm grip on the outlaw, looked questioningly at Senior.

'Where's George Adams?'

'Some of the Lovell people are taking care of him. He's conscious. They're taking him to the doc.'

'And the other outlaw?'

Senior smiled. 'I thought the easiest way to handle him was to put him to sleep. He's lying with his sidekick, under the trough.'

Then Seth was there, swinging down from the roan. A man in a dark suit came running from the bank; a crowd began to gather.

The man in the dark suit was pale in the face. His lips were trembling.

He said, 'The sons of bitches got nothing. There's precious little in the safe, just small change. It was the wrong time of the month for them, but by God it was the right time for us.'

Rafe looked at Crane. Blood was trickling down his neck. He was still unsteady on his feet; he was supporting himself with one hand on Rafe's shoulder. The ageing outlaw shook his head, and sucked in a ragged breath. He released his hold, took a step backwards and stood swaying. His face was impassive, but rage smouldered in his grey eyes.

'So much for the inside information you were promised,' Rafe said. 'Sangster sent you to the wrong bank.'

'We found that out the hard way,' the outlaw said, his voice tight. 'You and your brother are supposed to be smart, so now you tell me why Sangster would do that.'

But Rafe was already ahead of him,

his mind racing.

'Where was he when you left the canyon?'

'You mean where were they. Because another man was with him on the gallery when they watched us ride out, a man in an undertaker's black suit, wearing an undertaker's fancy string tie.'

'We know about him. His name's Kieran Stark, of the Wyoming Cattlemen's Association. You thought Sangster was behind this, but Stark was feeding him information and he's been dancing to Stark's tune. And I think you're beginning to realize what they've been doing.'

'Damn right. Sending six men to rob an empty safe sounds too familiar, too much like those diversionary tactics your brother was describing. You're here in Lovell gunning us down as we make damn fools of ourselves, Mort Sangster and that other character — '

'Are robbing a different bank,' Rafe said. 'The one where Joe Corrigan, for one, has almost certainly deposited a heap of money that's come from the sale of a big herd. But which bank are we talking about?'

'Not Alamo,' John Senior said. 'That's been done, and anyway it's the wrong area. I don't think any bank south of Lovell fits the bill. Fort Smith's too far north — and I'm not sure it's got a bank, anyway — so my educated guess is either Cowley or — '

He broke off as a moustachioed man wearing a badge pushed through the crowd. As a path was cleared for him, Rafe saw that another man with a badge was bending over the outlaw John Senior had left sleeping under the water trough.

A thin smile tugged at his lips at the Alamo lawman's deft and whimsical handling of a dangerous situation. He moved away and, as Senior set about bringing the Lovell marshal up to date with what had been going on, swung up behind Seth and crossed the square. A Lovell man rode to cut him off. He was leading Rafe's horse.

'That just about does it,' Seth said.

Rafe was back on his own horse. They were in the entrance to the alley, idly watching as the excitement died away.

'A couple of days ago your big idea was to stick around and clear our names,' Seth went on. 'That was done when we rode out of the canyon and reported back to Adams and Senior; told them the Alamo bank robbers were hiding in a lost valley with another four outlaws.'

'Sure. And we came here because it was on the way home. But this was just the first step. The next is Cowley.'

'So it seems. And here, if I'm not mistaken,' Seth said in amazement, 'comes the mighty figure of George Adams.'

Rafe couldn't believe his eyes. The Greybull marshal was approaching from the town side of the square astride his big chestnut gelding. He was holding his left arm rigidly close to his body, and the left side of his massive chest was made even larger by the bulk of the bandages just visible inside his shirt. Pain was naked in the lines of his face, but the big jaw was set firmly and an unquenchable spirit shone like a fiery beacon of hope in his eyes.

'Tell me what's been going on,' he said as he rode up. 'Make it short, make it fast, because I'm in no mood for long speeches. I know John Senior will be returning to Alamo — up in this neck of the woods he's way out of his jurisdiction. Besides, he's got his bank robbers — one live, one dead. OK. But while I was getting stitched up and amusing myself by swigging whiskey and biting on a grubby piece of stick, I was all the time urging the doc to hurry because I hated to think I was missing all the fun.'

'You're amazing, big man,' Rafe said with a shake of the head. 'But even you must have your limits, so tell me, are you up to a ride across the Shoshone, then on to Cowley?'

'Like you fellers, I could do with a

bath,' Adams said, 'and the first part of your question seems to put that right in an uncomfortable kind of way.' Clearly in pain, but still with all his wits about him, he cocked a knowing eyebrow. 'Are you telling me that somebody hit the wrong bank here in Lovell, and someone else is putting it right elsewhere?'

'That's about the size of it,' Rafe said. 'Point your horse towards the river, Marshal Adams, and we'll put you in the picture as we ride. We're going home, Seth and me, but if it becomes necessary we've no objection to giving an injured member of the law a helping hand along the way.'

# 17

They reached Cowley in the early afternoon. The heat that had begun to sap their strength in Lovell was made bearable by a cool breeze, picking up from the north and blowing in their faces as they rode in. George Adams was pale and drawn, but bearing his weakened condition and his pain with stoicism. And when they reached town it was he who led the way, pushing ahead over terrain familiar to him, leading the way without hesitation to yet another square.

They were on the edge of that square, slowing to survey a scene that was eerily familiar, when they were passed by another rider, a man who was driving his horse hard. He dragged a muttered curse from Seth as his horse kicked up a shower of dried mud, an exclamation of, 'Dammit, we're too late,' from Rafe as he watched the man hammer across the square and fling himself from his horse.

It was too late, in his opinion, because they had ridden twenty miles north but it was as if they had stepped back in time. The doors to another stone bank hung open. Another crowd had gathered, morbidly interested, and another grave man with a badge on his vest was down on one knee alongside a still figure whose blood was seeping into the dust.

'White hair, buckskin jacket, fancy boots,' Seth muttered. 'That man down on the ground is Sangster. He didn't make it — but where's Stark?'

The man bending over Mort Sangster picked up a white Stetson and placed it over the dead man's face, then stood up. He had about him an air of authority. Town marshal, Rafe thought; and it was that man that the rider who had just hammered into town approached. He was speaking loudly and excitedly to the lawman, embellishing his words with wild gestures. His words rang out clearly as George Adams led the Laramie brothers across the square to what they knew was the scene of another bank robbery.

'He headed north,' the excitable man said. 'Rode like the wind, then left the trail and disappeared in a spread of mesquite as tall as cottonwoods. After that, well, it's anybody's guess where he went, where he'll end up.'

'I'm willing to make that guess,' George Adams said. He nodded as the lawman turned to stare at him. 'Hello, Dave. Somebody walk in and make a cash withdrawal from your bank?'

'A big one, George.' The marshal walked over, reached up to shake Adams's hand. 'Your wife been giving you a hard time again, or did you fall off your horse?'

'One of these fine days we'll talk straight to each other,' Adams said, shaking his head. 'Fellers, meet George Harding, Cowley marshal and local wit.

George, these are the Laramie brothers, Rafe and Seth. They're on their way home from the war.'

'As it's now '67,' Harding said to Rafe, 'I'd say it's taking you an extraordinary long time.'

'Yeah, and these bank robberies are adding to the delay,' Rafe said. 'As to your question, well, George is a big man and most big men's wives always give them a hard time — '

'That's as maybe,' Adams said, 'and right or wrong I can live with it. However, how I got a bullet in the shoulder is another story — and it's long and complicated, Dave. The short of it is, this robbery's connected to one that went wrong in Lovell. It was meant to fail, but because it drew us in the wrong direction then, in a sense, it succeeded. The dead man you've just made decent, and the man who got away, were behind both.'

'I've got two deputies at the other end of town, drumming up a posse,' Harding said. 'If you have got an idea

218

where that feller's heading, I'd appreciate hearing it.'

'We-ell now, I don't think I can do that just yet,' Adams said, grimacing apologetically. 'Like I said, it didn't start here. Six men rode into my town and caused considerable chaos — '

'Where are they now?'

'One got away, two died, three are in custody — '

'Right, and you said the robbery failed so surely that's the end of it, for you. This is my town, my bank. Two men committed robbery. One died, the other got away with a heap of cash. If that money stays missing it will hurt several prominent ranchers, so my business is unfinished.'

'Then let us finish it for you.'

'No, you're way off your home range.'

'That's a moot point, Dave, when it comes to hunting down law-breakers. Besides, you don't know where I'll finish up, because you don't know where Stark is heading.'

'North. You heard the man. That takes him even further out of your jurisdiction.'

'And yours too, Marshal,' Rafe pointed out.

Dave Harding's face was bleak. He turned away, walked a couple of paces. Then he stopped, and swung around with a frown creasing his brow.

'Stark, you say?' he said, pensively. 'I know of only one fellow called Stark. First name Kieran. Got a top position with the Cattlemen's Association.' He looked hard at Adams. 'Are we talking about the same man?'

Adams nodded. 'Ruthless men have a habit of treading on toes — that's how they reach power, that's how they remain at the top. But sometimes their hold is precarious. Stark's hanging on by his fingernails. He needs something else. Looks like this was it.'

Harding said nothing. He was looking beyond Adams, his eyes on some distant horizon, but Rafe could see that his mind was working on complications he hadn't foreseen. Then the marshal shook his head angrily.

'All right,' he said. 'If you know where he is, go get him. But if you've got it wrong about Stark and you dig yourself into a hole you can't get out of,' he added with a wicked, mirthless smile, 'make damn sure you keep the name Dave Harding well out of it.'

# 18

Once again the foreman was there in the yard when, late in the afternoon, Kieran Stark rode into the Circle C. Stark noticed at once that the big, raw-boned cowboy had the sheen of sweat on his forehead and was slapping dust from his clothes as he moved to meet him.

*A big herd has been sold,* Stark thought. *This man will have been working hard with his crew, moving the cattle to their new owner.* And he allowed himself a thin smile at the thought that if everything went according to plan then, within minutes, the Circle C itself would be changing hands and the foreman would be out of a job.

The foreman, however, was also looking smug — and that, and the look in the man's level grey eyes, gave Stark a fleeting moment of concern. Then, as on the previous occasion, he was invited by the foreman to step down from his horse. But this time there were two differences: when Stark dismounted and strode into the big house for what he knew would be his last meeting with Joe Corrigan, he carried with him two bulging saddle-bags; and when he entered the rancher's front room, he was closely followed by the big foreman.

The oversized, shabby armchair was empty. Joe Corrigan was sitting behind an expensive desk. His eyes were cold and watchful, the fingers of his veined hands laced. No drink was offered to Stark. The foreman moved silently to a position against the wall. The butt of his six-gun bumped against the wood panels.

Joe Corrigan smiled thinly at the sound, and shook his head. Then he turned his gaze on Stark.

'So, once again you call on me wearing that greedy look I have grown accustomed to. Are you expecting a different answer this time, Mr Stark?'

'Sure I am.'

With a swift movement, Stark dumped the two saddle-bags on the desk in front of Corrigan. They landed with a thump. Papers fluttered to the floor. An ash tray clattered.

'And we both know why,' he said, stepping back. 'Your herd's gone, sold, moved out, which makes your continued ownership of this ranch look ridiculous. And there, on your desk, is the money I offered, and a good deal more to sweeten the deal.'

'Well, well,' Corrigan said softly. He flashed a look at the foreman. 'What d'you think of that, Kent?'

The foreman stirred, eased his position.

'I think he's a slimy sonofabitch. But even sons of bitches talk sense from time to time. I think it's a good offer.'

'Lots of offers have been good. Why should I take this one?'

'He's offering you too much cash for a property without stock. That's foolish.

Accepting the offer would be sensible — and you always were a sensible man. But you need to move fast, before he changes his mind.'

Corrigan chuckled.

'Always assuming he's got a mind to change,' he said. Then he leaned forward and placed both hands possessively on the saddle-bags. 'All right, Mr Stark, you've got yourself a deal. Kent, take these out, put them somewhere safe.'

As a hot tide of elation flooded through him, Stark stepped to one side. Kent, the foreman, brushed past and swept the saddle-bags from the desk. The door banged behind him as he left the room.

Corrigan looked at Stark. He sat back in his chair. One eyebrow was raised, as if he was waiting for Stark to speak.

Stark obliged. His throat felt thick, clogged. He could hardly believe his luck.

'You've got your money, Corrigan,'

he said huskily. 'All it needs to complete the deal is for you to move out.'

'Oh, I've already arranged that,' Corrigan said blandly.

Stark, nodded — then frowned, as his mind grasped the meaning behind the rancher's words.

'What . . . you've already arranged it? Are you saying you expected me here today, had decided to accept my offer before I walked in?'

'Oh no. My imminent move has nothing to do with you, Mr Stark. I'm moving because I no longer own this ranch. The Circle C is not mine.'

'Well, yes, I *know* that. I've just *bought* the place, every building, every acre.'

Corrigan shook his head. 'No, you haven't. The Circle C was sold some time before you got here, Mr Stark. It was sold to a successful Wyoming rancher as a going concern: buildings, land, and stock. All you've done is given me back my own money.'

'Your money?'

'Yes. It's remarkable, isn't it, but coincidences do happen. Kent was in town today; in Cowley. There was a bank robbery — but of course, you know that.'

'Do I?' Stark said hoarsely.

'Kent was a witness. He saw one man die, the other get away. So he followed that man — at a discreet distance. He had a fair idea where that man was going, of course. And when he was absolutely sure, he rode past him — again, at a distance that ensured he was not seen.'

Stunned, unable to speak, Stark stumbled backwards. His mind was in turmoil. It was as if he could feel the weight of the saddle-bags in his hands, the heft that was all cash — and he had given them away, given it away — every last dollar, every last greenback. If he could get it back, if he could go after the foreman . . .

He turned away from the desk, his hand fumbling for his six-gun.

'I think I should advise you,'

Corrigan said pleasantly, 'that the move you are contemplating is unwise. If you look out of the window, you will see that three horsemen have entered the yard. Kent is with them, no doubt telling them what he saw in town, and what has happened here. My eyes are not as sharp as they once were, but I believe one of those men is wearing a badge.'

★   ★   ★

They remained on their horses, not knowing if Stark would emerge from the front of the house or make his break from the rear on a stolen horse. They were amused by the foreman's tale; impressed by the old rancher's handling of the situation; scornful of Stark's stupidity.

But what would he do next?

'He's coming out,' Rafe Laramie said.

'If he's got sense, he'll come out with his hands up,' Seth said.

'Sense has got damn all to do with it,' said George Adams. 'If he had sense he wouldn't have done what he did and we wouldn't be here. He'll come out with guns blazing, that's all he *can* do — '

The front door was jerked open. Kieran Stark exploded onto the gallery. He leaped to one side. Dropped to a crouch. Then he opened up with his drawn six-gun. He fired twice, three times. The bullets flew high and wide.

Then, coolly, casually, George Adams lifted his six-gun and shot Kieran Stark in the chest. The heavy slug knocked him back against the wall. He hit hard. Then he slid down to lie in a crumpled heap.

'And that,' Adams said, 'is that.' He grinned at the Laramie brothers. 'It's over, fellers — and I guess now, at last, you can go home.

We do hope that you have enjoyed reading this large print book.

Did you know that all of our titles are available for purchase?

We publish a wide range of high quality large print books including:
**Romances, Mysteries, Classics**
**General Fiction**
**Non Fiction and Westerns**

Special interest titles available in large print are:
**The Little Oxford Dictionary**
**Music Book, Song Book**
**Hymn Book, Service Book**

Also available from us courtesy of Oxford University Press:
**Young Readers' Dictionary**
**(large print edition)**
**Young Readers' Thesaurus**
**(large print edition)**

For further information or a free brochure, please contact us at:
**Ulverscroft Large Print Books Ltd.,**
**The Green, Bradgate Road, Anstey,**
**Leicester, LE7 7FU, England.**
**Tel:** (00 44) 0116 236 4325
**Fax:** (00 44) 0116 234 0205

## GUNSLINGER BREED

### Corba Sunman

Gunslinger Clint Halloran rides into Plainsville to help his pal Jeff Deacon, hoping to end his friend's troubles. But Deacon is on the point of being lynched, so he fires a shot. Now Halloran has a fight on his hands, a situation complicated by the crooked deputy sheriff, Dan Ramsey, who has his own agenda. Halloran, refusing to give up the fight, vows to keep his gun by his side — right until the final shot is fired.

# DEAD END TRAIL

## Tyler Hatch

Chet Rand is a decent, law-abiding man, but a forest fire wipes out his horse ranch, leaving him with nothing. However, when he comes across the outlaw Feeney — with a $1,100 reward on his head — it seems like a gift from heaven. Unfortunately, there are many shady characters in pursuit of the $12,000 Feeney has stolen — a more pressing matter than the bounty itself. So it's inevitable that when guns are drawn, blood will flow and men will die . . .

# DUEL AT DEL NORTE

## Ethan Flagg

Russ Wikeley settles in Del Norte, South Dakota, and after foiling a bank robbery he's persuaded to stand for sheriff in the town's elections. However, Diamond Jim Stoner, a gang boss, wants his own man to become sheriff and attempts to undermine Wikeley. When his plan backfires, he tries to frame his adversary for robbery and murder. Both men are determined . . . only one can be the victor in the final duel on the streets of Del Norte.

# THE KILLING KIND

## Lance Howard

Jim Bartlett thought he could put his past behind him and forge a new life in Texas, as a small ranch owner — but he was wrong ... dead wrong. Someone from his past has followed him and is systematically trying to destroy his new life, piece by piece. With his friends and the woman he loves being threatened by a man who knows no remorse, Jim struggles desperately — not only to escape his past — but also to hold onto his life ...